THE BIG EMPTY

Stan Jones and Patricia Watts

SOHO
CRIME

Published by
Soho Press, Inc.
853 Broadway
New York, NY 10003

Library of Congress Cataloging-in-Publication Data
Jones, Stan | Watts, Patricia
The big empty / Stan Jones and Patricia Watts.

I. Title
PS3560.O539 B54 2018 813'.54—dc23 2018027721

ISBN 978-1-64129-002-9
eISBN 978-1-64129-003-6

Interior design by Janine Agro, Soho Press, Inc.

Printed in the United States of America

10 9 8 7 6 5 4 3 2 1

To Laura Hruska

THE BIG EMPTY

A NOTE ON LANGUAGE

"Eskimo" is the best-known term for the Native Americans described in this book, but it is not their term. In their own language, they call themselves Inupiat, meaning the People. "Eskimo," which was brought into Alaska by white men, is what certain Indian tribes in eastern Canada called their neighbors to the north. It most likely meant "eaters of raw flesh."

Nonetheless, "Eskimo" and "Inupiat" are used more or less interchangeably in Northwest Alaska today, at least when English is spoken, and that is the usage followed in this book.

But this usage may be changing. In 2016, the federal government decided to eliminate the term "Eskimo" from its own documents, and the authentic and indigenous "Inupiat" seems to be gradually superseding it, especially among younger and better-educated members of the culture.

The term "Inuit" is sometimes proposed as a replacement for

"Eskimo" in collective reference to the many branches of the cultural tree known as the Eskimos. But some Alaskan Inupiat reject "Inuit" in application to themselves. They argue—accurately—that it is a Canadian term referring to Canadian Eskimos and should not be applied to American Eskimos.

The imported "Eskimo" remains very much in use in Northwest Alaska. As depicted in an exchange partway through this book, it is sometimes regarded as the cultural property of today's Inupiat, used only within the group itself as a kind of ironic armor against white prejudice. Other times, it seems instead to reflect the internalizing of that prejudice. Such usage also appears in this book, as when one of the characters refers to himself as a "dumb Eskimo."

NORTHWEST ALASKA GLOSSARY

aaka **(AH-kuh):** mother

aana **(AH-nuh):** old lady, grandmother

akkaga **(uh-KAH-guh):** uncle

anaq **(AH-nuk):** feces

angatquq **(AHNG-ut-cook):** shaman

arigaa **(AH-de-gah):** it's good

arii **(ah-DEE):** ouch, it hurts

attata **(uh-TAH-ta):** grandfather

atiqluk **(AH-tee-cluck):** a woman's hooded overshirt, often of flowered fabric, with a large front pocket

bunnik **(BUN-nuk):** affectionate term for daughter. The actual Inupiaq word is *paniq*.

Eskimo (as a verb): to improvise a solution on the spot, from available materials, often in a way requiring considerable ingenuity. The closest English analog is probably "MacGyver."

Inupiaq (IN-you-pyock): one Eskimo; the Eskimo language

Inupiat (IN-you-pat): more than one Inupiaq; the Eskimo people

kunnichuk **(KUH-nee-chuck):** Arctic entry, or vestibule

kuukuung **(koo-KOONG):** affectionate term for a small child, comparable to "punkin" in English

malik **(MULL-uck):** follow or accompany

naluaqmiiyaaq **(nuh-LOCK-me-ock):** an Inupiaq who puts on airs and acts almost white

naluaqmiu, naluaqmiut **(nuh-LOCK-me):** white person, white race

pamiuktuk **(PUH-me-UCK-tuck):** otter

quiyuk **(KWEE-uck):** sex

sheefish: a delicious freshwater whitefish that can reach sixty pounds in weight

taaqsipak **(TOX-ee-puck):** the color black; an African American

ulu **(OO-loo):** traditional Eskimo woman's knife, shaped like a slice of pizza with the cutting edge at the rim

uqpik **(OOK-pick):** willow

Village English: a stripped-down form of English used by the Inupiat of Northwest Alaska, particularly older people and residents of small villages

Yoi (yoy): so lucky

THE BIG EMPTY

PROLOGUE

"Son of a bitch."

Nathan Active jerked upright in the Navajo's copilot seat at the sudden sound of Cowboy Decker's bush-pilot drawl in the headset. He pulled his gaze in from the terrain off the plane's right wing and peered over the nose at the ridge ahead.

Had he dozed off? It had been a struggle to stay alert during the ninety-minute flight through the granite ridges and green-carpeted valleys of the Brooks Range. He had been up most of the previous night arresting Ernie Beaver, drunk again on homebrew, for administering another beating to his equally drunk girlfriend. And, also as usual, arresting the girlfriend when she waded in with an *ulu* to defend her man from the cops. Standard domestic violence case. At least they'd become less frequent since Chukchi had outlawed liquor a few years earlier.

Cowboy's voice came again. "See? Up from that patch of brush there, maybe a hundred feet below the crest?"

A honey-brown ripple caught Active's eye—sunlight glinting off a grizzly in summer coat, ambling through a snarl of alders in a gully that slashed down the face of the ridge. And just above that, Cessna 207 parts splattered across the hillside like bugs on a windshield.

Cowboy swung the Navajo parallel to the ridge and Active studied the crash site as it flashed past.

The impact had separated the tail and wings from the fuselage, which was crumpled but looked to be still attached to the engine. The propeller blades were bent back and the landing gear was splayed out, though still attached to the fuselage. So were both doors of the cockpit, though the windshield was gone. Active was glad he couldn't see inside.

"Son of a bitch," Cowboy said again.

"Any doubt it's them?"

Cowboy dropped the flaps, backed off the throttles, and slowed the Navajo to its minimum safe airspeed, then rolled into a wide, easy arc over the sun-splashed valley below the ridge for another pass. "Of course it's them. That's my plane, and—well, shit. That's Evie's hat. See there, that little speck of orange? She never climbed in an airplane without it."

Active squinted and finally picked up the tiny patch of color a few yards from the fuselage. Maybe it was a hat, maybe not. "Sorry, buddy."

"Her lucky hat, she called it." The pilot's shoulders were shaking. "Those kids. I, I . . ."

Active let the silence run on as Cowboy made another circle. He had ridden with Evie Kavoonah at the controls on a couple of village cases. He remembered bright eyes and a kind of innate merriness that he had come to associate with the Inupiat, especially Inupiat women.

"No way we can land, right?" he said at last.

"Not in a Navajo, not around here. Search and Rescue will have to bring in a helicopter to recover the bod—to get them out."

It was what Active had expected. The Navajo was big and fast, with two engines, the queen of the Lienhofer Aviation fleet and perfect for an air search 150 miles out of Chukchi. But it was no bush plane. It needed a long, smooth runway.

"They'll want confirmation, I suppose," Active said.

Cowboy grunted assent. "I'll bring you past again. See if you can get the tail number."

Active pulled his Nikon from the case between his knees. "I'll get some pictures, too."

They made the pass. Active got his pictures and noted the Cessna's registration number, then Cowboy pushed the throttles forward and hauled back on the yoke. The engines roared, the Navajo's nose pointed up at the cloud-flecked sky, and Cowboy got on the radio to report their find. "Catastrophic damage," Active heard him tell the FAA back in Chukchi. "Not survivable."

"You need to check the pictures?" Active asked when they were level and the engines had slowed to the steady thrum of cruise power.

"No, thanks," Cowboy said. "I never want to see that again."

After a long time, he spoke once more. "I don't think I ever saw her without that hat. She said she wouldn't take it off even for a kiss from a hot guy. She told me she knew Todd was the one when it flew off by itself the first time she saw him."

Active could think of no words to ease the pain, so he didn't speak.

"They were both so young," Cowboy muttered as the remains of Two-Five-Mike vanished behind them.

CHAPTER ONE

• *Wednesday, August 17* •

LIENHOFER AVIATION, CHUKCHI

Active followed the smell of stale cigarette smoke and day-old coffee down a grimy hallway to the break room on the second floor of Lienhofer Aviation's hangar and terminal at the Chukchi airport. He had been driving to Arctic Pizza to meet Grace for lunch when Cowboy's urgent call came in.

He found the pilot at a chipped Formica table with his back to a picture window that overlooked the tarmac and the airport's main runway.

"What's the emergency?" Active crossed the room and pulled out an orange vinyl chair.

Cowboy slid a stack of papers across the table, knocking over a half-full can of Coke in the process. Brown foam swirled across the floor. "You seen this yet?"

Active righted the can, picked up the papers, and scanned what turned out to be the official report on the Cessna 207 crash that had killed Evie Kavoonah and Todd Brenner six weeks earlier.

"No, I—"

"Ah, why would you? It just came out." Cowboy shoved back his chair and paced in front of the window. He pulled off his Lienhofer ball cap, returned it to his head, put on his mirrored shades, and snatched them off again. His sun-browned face was unshaven. His eyes were red, and the crow's feet at the corners showed a little deeper than they should have on a man in his mid-forties. He groped inside his weathered bomber jacket, came up with a pack of Marlboros, and tapped one out.

Active looked up from the report as Cowboy brought the cigarette to his lips, lit it with a red Bic, and took a drag.

His own face looked back at him from Cowboy's lenses. Active ran his hand over the bristly buzz cut that made him look closer to twenty than thirty. "Pilot error, huh? Tough one, I guess."

"And total bullshit." The cigarette bobbed. "That girl was the most meticulous pilot I ever flew with. I gave her her first lesson when she was thirteen, and even then she had more airplane sense than a lot of pros my age."

Active read from the report. "'Probable cause of this accident was the pilot's failure to confirm the aircraft had adequate fuel on board to complete the flight.'" He dropped it on the Formica table. "She ran out of gas."

"Not Evie. Do you know the meaning of 'meticulous'?"

"Of course, but"—Active looked at the report again—"but this says, 'no fuel was observed in the lines, and propeller damage was consistent with the engine not producing power at impact.'"

"No way she ran out of gas," Cowboy said. "I checked those tanks myself that morning while she was doing her preflight. They were full, right up to the filler neck. And with full tanks, Two-Five-Mike could fly the 440 miles to Fairbanks and most of the way back."

Outside the window, a red and white Cessna 207 lifted off into a cloudless sky and banked east, presumably for a trip to the villages up the Isignaq River.

Active flipped through the report again. "So the weather was clear here that day and clear in Fairbanks, but there was cloud cover in between?"

"Yeah, a cold front was sliding through, but it wasn't a problem."

Cowboy tapped ash from his cigarette into the empty Coke can and stepped up to the big aviation chart on the wall.

"What we do in a case like that is, we climb out of Chukchi and get on top of the clouds." Cowboy swept a hand across the jumble of rivers, ridges, peaks, and tundra plateaus that lay between Chukchi and the Yukon River to the south. "So Evie would have been above the weather till she got to the other side, then they were gonna stop at Tanana for lunch and a potty break. From there, it was a sightseeing run up the Tanana River into Fairbanks. It's a beautiful ride in decent weather."

"Sounds like it."

"We do it all the time. In fact, I flew that route with her back in April to show her the ropes. Same kind of weather, too."

The pilot dropped into his chair and massaged his eyes. "I was supposed to go this time, too—I was having the radios upgraded—and Todd was gonna ride along. Then he and Evie decided they needed to make a trip to Fairbanks, all of a sudden they had to look for an engagement ring. And they wanted to see a specialist over there about the baby. So I let them take Two-Five-Mike."

"Specialist? Was there a problem with the pregnancy?"

They fell silent as a skinny Inupiaq in his thirties wearing grease-stained Carhartts and a backward baseball cap wandered in. He exchanged nods with Cowboy, shot a curious glance at Active in his uniform, then poured the last of the acrid-smelling coffee into a chipped mug decorated with a cartoon moose and shuffled out.

"So," Active continued. "Problem pregnancy?"

"Evie's mom had a couple of miscarriages," Cowboy said. "So they weren't taking any chances. They were both like that, always double-checking everything. I trusted Evie with that airplane a hundred and ten percent. And she would have been extra careful because of that baby."

He pulled the Marlboro from his lips and studied it absently. "I shoulda gone with them, you know? Maybe I could have found a way down through those clouds." He smiled, a faraway look in his eyes. "Evie used to tell me I didn't fly that plane, I wore it."

"Maybe you could have done it," Active said. "Maybe not. Maybe nobody could have."

Cowboy looked thoughtful for a while. Then he picked up the report and studied it. Finally he jabbed at it with the Marlboro. "It just doesn't make sense."

"All right, take me through it. So, Evie was a careful pilot."

"Meticulous, like I said."

"You were upgrading the radios. They on the fritz?"

"No, they were fine," Cowboy said. "But they were getting old, couldn't do all the stuff the new ones do. It's just something you have to deal with every few years when you own a plane in commercial service."

"If they were working, wouldn't she have called in before she went down?"

"Not necessarily. You get into trouble, you go into A-N-C mode."

"A-N-C?"

"Aviate, Navigate, Communicate. First, you aviate—fly the airplane. Second, you navigate—keep track of where you are. And, third, you communicate—call in if you have time. Evie was trying to restart a dead engine and not hit any of the mountains she knew were in those clouds, so she never got around to communicating."

"This report says the engine wasn't producing power when they went down. But let's say the feds are wrong and she didn't run out of gas. Then what was it? Something break?"

Cowboy's jaw took on a stubborn set. "No way. That was my airplane. I'm the only mechanic to work on it since I bought it twelve years ago."

Active was silent, feeling for an easy way into it. There wasn't one, he concluded. "Could you have missed something?"

"No."

"Maybe something wasn't exactly in top condition, but you figured it would hold together till you got around to it?"

Cowboy froze in mid-stride. "Fuck you, Nathan." He flipped the cigarette butt toward the garbage can in the corner next to the refrigerator. He missed.

"Sorry." Active waited for Cowboy to pick up the cigarette. He didn't. "I'm just trying to consider every possib—"

"I wouldn't let those kids anywhere near that plane if it wasn't rock-solid." Cowboy sagged back into the chair and rocked it onto its rear legs and was silent for a time.

"Shit. Could I have missed something?"

"All we've got is this report."

"No, dammit!" The chair's front feet banged onto the floor. "There was nothing wrong with Two-Five-Mike. If it ran out of gas, somebody jimmied the fuel system."

"What? You mean sabotage?"

The pilot met Active's gaze without flinching.

"Seriously?" Active said.

A stocky Inupiaq with a scraggly goatee and a Crazy Eskimo ball cap rolled a squeaky-wheeled gray trash bin through the doorway. Again they waited the new arrival out.

The janitor pulled the overflowing plastic bag out of the garbage, closed it with a zip tie, and tossed it into his bin. Then he spotted the soda spill, mopped it up and cleaned the spot, and wheeled his bin out again.

"All I know is, I checked those tanks myself that morning," Cowboy said. "Like I said, Two-Five-Mike had enough gas to get to Fairbanks and most of the way back. And that plane wouldn't just quit. And that leaves sabotage."

"Cowboy—"

"I'm gonna prove it."

"Prove it? How? If the federal investigators didn't—"

"The evidence is on that ridge. I'm gonna go up there and find it."

The phone in Active's pocket warbled. He pulled it out, tapped the screen, and put it to his ear. "Hey, baby. Yeah, I'm sorry, I can't right now . . . All right, yeah, right. See you tonight. Me too."

"Some drama with mama?"

"Not how I would put it, but yeah. That's the third time today she's called. I haven't had time to talk to her, and now I've stood her up for lunch. I'm sure I'll hear about it when I get home."

"Ya think?" Cowboy slid down in the chair, a little looser and more relaxed now. "So are you gonna help me figure this out or what?"

"It's a plane crash. If it was sabotage, which I seriously doubt, I'm pretty sure that's under federal juris—"

"I already called the FBI. They looked up the crash report and called back to say they're not interested."

Active studied his friend. How to get him off of the idea? "I can't start a murder investigation with no evidence, no motive, and no weapon. The feds had a whole team of experts—"

"Team? Ha!" Cowboy spat it out like an olive pit. He heaved up from the chair, and started pacing again. "The 'team' was two guys, and they got yanked off the crash site when that commuter flight augered in at Dutch Harbor. What I think? A personal flight, no obvious cause, bureaucrats with workload issues, you take the path of least resistance, call it pilot error, and presto! Case closed."

Active cocked his head and eyed Cowboy. A murder investigation on a mountainside 150 miles into the wilderness, with a grief-crazed bush pilot in charge? It was ridiculous. The logistics alone . . .

Cowboy stopped pacing and faced him. "Please?"

Active sighed. He smelled the scorched dregs of the emptied coffee pot on the burner and the piney scent of the cleaner the janitor had used on the soda spill.

"Is the wreckage still up there?"

"I overflew it yesterday," Cowboy said. "As far as I could tell, the feds didn't cart anything off. Probably too expensive, considering the distance and the terrain."

"Doesn't your insurance company own it now?"

"Nah, I bought it from them after they settled the claim. They were only too happy to be off the hook for a salvage operation in the wilderness. And somebody might have mentioned something about grizzlies being known to frequent the area."

"How close can you land up there?" Active asked.

"Not too far. There's a gravel bar down on the river with a slough where I can drop in my new floatplane."

"Not too far? How far is that?"

"Ah, a little hike. A mile maybe."

"But uphill, right?"

"Not coming back," Cowboy said.

"And when you get up there, you're going to do what, exactly?"

"Take that airplane apart, piece by piece."

Active took the report from the pilot and scanned it again. "Okay, Cowboy. I have some vacation coming up, so if we time it right, I can go. If we find evidence of foul play, I'll look into it. But if not, we're done. I'll have to drop it, and so will you. Right?"

Cowboy nodded, sank back into the chair, and exhaled. "Thanks, Nathan. Thanks."

CHAPTER TWO

• *Wednesday, August 17* •

HOME OF NATHAN AND GRACE ACTIVE, CHUKCHI

Active pulled his blue and white Chevy Tahoe up to the rented three-bedroom house set on steel pilings over the lagoon behind Chukchi. It had been home since he and Grace had married the previous spring, and was typical of Chukchi in its lack of pretense. No lawn, no real driveway, just a patch of gravel thrown down on the tundra at the back door. It did have a front door that opened onto a deck on the lagoon side, which was nice for morning coffee in the summer.

He watched from the SUV as a little flotilla of ducks patrolled the slate-surfaced water near the pilings. Drizzle speckled the windshield. Two quarreling seagulls circled Nita's fishing net strung across the water fifty yards from shore.

He pictured Grace inside, cutting up vegetables and baking a salmon from Nita's catch. Nita would be sprawled across the pink and yellow cover of her bed, playing *Never Alone* on her laptop.

The game about the adventures of an Inupiat girl named Nuna and her Arctic fox was all the rage for teenage girls in Chukchi lately.

How to break the news that he was calling off their long-awaited expedition up the Katonak River to climb a ridge in the middle of nowhere and dig through a plane crash with Cowboy Decker? He and Grace certainly needed the time together. She had been moody with pregnancy hormones for weeks, elated one moment, paralyzed with dread the next.

It wasn't complicated for him. He was already imagining the first fishing trip with his son—*his* son. Not that they knew the sex yet, but in his fantasy it was a boy, always a boy.

They had argued about it again the night before and ended with her saying, as always, "It's just not simple for me." Then she retreated into herself and he knew it was useless to try to talk to her or touch her for the rest of the night.

Female behavior, he had learned, could be like one of Chukchi's howling winter blizzards. About all you could do was hunker down and ride it out. At least the makeup sex that morning had gone right, so maybe the storm had passed.

He swung down from the Tahoe and took a deep breath.

Grace caught him at the door, circled his waist, and almost knocked him down. He inhaled lavender from her skin. "What's all this?" he asked. "Was I that good this morning?"

He drew back to study her face, the clear, honey skin, the high cheekbones. Those quicksilver eyes brimming above her smile.

"You were great, my checkup went great, and I'm just . . . happy, I guess."

"Me too, then." He hoisted her in the air, swung her around, and kissed her.

She pulled away and walked into the kitchen. He sensed the hormones had flipped again.

He moved behind her as she leaned on the counter, head bowed.

"But . . . not totally happy?"

"I still don't know if I can do it. I mean, I want it for you, but I don't know if I'm strong enough, and—"

He turned her to face him. "And?"

"And Nita's father was my father. And I had to give her up to Aunt Aggie to raise as her own. And she doesn't know I'm her mother. She can't ever know."

The words came tumbling out in the familiar rush that meant she was speaking more to herself now than to him. He thought of trying to stop it, but knew better from experience. Once she started down that back trail, the dark history always lurking at the edge of her consciousness would spill out until it was done.

"And then there was the other lifetime I spent on the street in Anchorage selling myself to any guy with a bottle of Bacardi," she was saying.

"But this is now," he tried. "That was then."

"But it's still inside me. And I can't make it go away." Tears spilled down her cheeks. "What's wrong with me?"

He drew her into his arms and stroked her shining black hair.

What's wrong with me? How often had he heard that? For such a long time, the ghost of her father had kept her from taking him inside her when they made love. *What's wrong with me?* she would say. But they had made do with hands and lips and patience, until one night it had happened in a sheefish camp on the ice of Chukchi Bay. Her face that first time had been like a sunrise.

"Nothing's wrong with you, Grace."

"Yeah, right." She pushed him back. "We're having a baby . . . and I can't even . . . I don't—"

"If it takes us a little longer to work things out, that just makes it extra great, right? When the time comes, we'll have the fruit of all our labors."

She swiped at the tears and grinned a little. "Only I'm the one that has to carry the fruit and go through the labor."

"Hey, we're doing it together. Remember?"

"Yeah, that's how we got ourselves into this fix." They shared a smile of relief for a second: she was herself again. "But, what about after the baby is born? What kind of mother will I be?"

"You're doing a fine job with Nita."

"Yeah, for now. But maybe that's just thanks to my aunt raising her for the first ten years of her life. Maybe it's just a matter of time before I blow this up. What do I know about raising a girl?"

"Maybe it's a boy."

"Somehow, I doubt that would be any easier. But Nita might prefer a little brother."

"Have you told her?"

"No. The only new family member she's expecting is a dog."

"A dog?"

"She showed me this picture of a puppy her friend Stacy is giving away. Maybe we can talk about it over dinner." She pulled plates from the cupboard and set them around the table as Active retrieved forks and knives from the dish drainer in the sink. "Maybe I'll tell her while we're all camping."

Active hadn't figured out how to break the news about the trip with Cowboy, so he tried a diversion.

"Let's not wait," he said. "We don't want her to feel like we kept it from her."

"Maybe you're right, maybe we should tell her tonight so she can process for a couple days, then we can just relax and enjoy ourselves in camp this weekend. We're almost packed."

Apparently there was no way around it. "Uh-huh, about that, um—"

"No." Her eyes were wide. "No! Do not tell me you have to work. I've got Dolly lined up to fill in for me at the shelter, and Nita is back in school next week."

"No, not work exactly. Remember that plane crash last month?"

"You mean Evie Kavoonah and that doctor in Cowboy's plane?"

"Yeah. Todd Brenner. Cowboy was really close to them, especially to Evie. She was like the daughter he and his wife never had. And Evie and Todd had just found out they were having a baby."

Grace winced and put a hand over her stomach.

"The feds are calling it pilot error, but Cowboy doesn't buy it," Active said. "He thinks if we go up there and crawl through the wreckage, we might—well, we might find something."

"Like what?"

"Like sabotage."

"Wait. Cowboy thinks—?"

Active nodded.

"And you?"

"I think it's a wild goose chase. I think Cowboy's in denial because he taught Evie to fly. He's afraid he forgot something— afraid it killed her and Todd. Or that he screwed up the maintenance on that plane and that's what killed them."

Active broke eye contact and concentrated on wiping the water spots off a glass on the cluttered kitchen counter.

"Seriously? You're passing up three days of fishing and hunting and berry picking with your two favorite girls, two nights in a sleeping bag with your snuggle bunny, just because—"

"If you could have seen him in my office . . . I never saw him look like that before. Like an *aana* when her granddaughter goes missing, or a father when I ask him the whereabouts of the good boy who couldn't possibly have killed his girlfriend."

"But sabotage? In Chukchi?"

"Exactly," Active said. "Who in this town is going to sabotage a bush plane? And why? But Cowboy won't let it go."

"I see this with the women at the shelter every day—rationalizing and denial. It's a common way of coping with abuse. They can't heal till they accept reality. If you go along with this, aren't you just enabling him?"

Active turned it over in his mind. He backed away so she could set the food on the table.

"He's going regardless. He'll dig through that wreckage for what isn't there. And when he comes face to face with the fact that sometimes people we love die and we'll never know why, or worse, if he finds out that somehow he caused that crash, I don't know what he'll do. I think I have to be there to catch him when he falls. He's really in trouble."

Grace studied his face, then took it between her hands and kissed him. "You're so *you*, Nathan Active. When do you leave?"

"Friday."

"I'll help you pack. One condition, though."

He tilted his head, a wary grin on his face.

"You explain this to Nita."

He nodded. "I'll make it up to you." He returned the kiss.

"I'm hungry," Nita's voice interrupted from the kitchen door.

"She emerges!" Active shot the girl a grin.

"Wash your hands?" Grace asked.

Nita rolled her eyes and headed for the bathroom.

"Speaking of food, do you need supplies, or are you and Cowboy going to survive on beans and pilot bread?"

"There's a river close to the crash site where we'll land and probably camp on a gravel bar to get away from the bugs. We could fish, but I don't think we'll have much time for that, so, yeah. Beans, Tang, pilot bread, Mountain House. And, of course, peanut butter."

Grace smiled. "Hm."

"What?"

"You're gonna need a camp crew."

"Ah, I see where you're going with this. I don't know—"

"Oh, Nita and I are absolutely gonna *malik* you. We'll fish and cook, maybe shoot a caribou, pick blueberries—the ladies at work say they're lots and good right now—and we'll still have our vacation. Kind of."

"I'll have to check with Cowb—"

"Good. It's settled, then. Visions of blueberries are dancing in my head. Buckets and buckets of blueberries."

"Not to mention mosquitoes. Billions and billions of mosquitoes."

"Which is why God made bug dope and head nets. There's no way you are leaving me and Nita alone this weekend."

"And grizzlies, according to Cowboy."

"Which is why God made the Winchester .308."

"But, I mean, with the baby and all."

"Like I'd take some kind of risk? Because I don't want it as much as you do?" She slid past him without another word.

"Hey, I didn't mean it like—I only meant—"

The door slammed as she went out onto the deck.

Nita came into the kitchen, sat down, and dished salmon and yellow squash onto a plate. "Where's Mom?"

"She went outside for a minute."

"For what?"

"Needed some air, I guess. Listen, I hear your friend has a puppy to give away."

"Yeah," Nita said around a mouthful of dinner. "My friend Stacy."

"What kind of puppy does she have?"

"He. Stacy's a boy."

"Cute?"

Nita blushed and lowered her eyes.

"I meant the puppy."

"Nathan!" Grace's voice called from outside.

He and Nita exchanged a look.

"Sounds like you better go," the girl said.

"Uh-huh."

Active found her at the railing overlooking the lagoon, still except for a lock of hair that fluttered a little with the wind. Her eyebrows were beaded from the rain that pattered down.

"Look," she murmured.

He followed her gaze across the lagoon. A double rainbow arced through the misty sky over the tundra bluffs east of town.

He put an arm around her waist. She leaned into his shoulder. He spread his fingers on her belly. They were both silent for a time.

Then she spoke. "Didn't someone say life is what happens while you're busy making other plans?"

"You mean the trip?"

She took a deep breath. "And the baby." She turned to look at him. "Let's go have that talk with Nita."

CHAPTER THREE

• Friday, August 19 – Saturday, August 20 •

Hawk River Valley, Brooks Range

"Is Mom sick?" Nita asked. "Why did she say smelling raw fish made her want to throw up?"

Active glanced back at the girl, crouched in a turquoise and lavender *atiqluk* and wielding an *ulu* as she filleted an arctic char.

Something hit Active's Dardevle lure and another big char broke the surface of the river. He yanked back on his spinning rod to set the treble hook. The fish arched its back and rolled on its side as he fought it toward the gravel.

"Sometimes pregnant women have morning sickness," he answered as he worked the char in.

"But it's not morning."

"Leave it to your mom to have afternoon sickness. Or maybe she's a little queasy from the flight."

It was possible. Cowboy had swooped across the ridge where the mangled remains of the 207 awaited them, then jolted down through a crosswind to splash his new blue and white Cessna float-plane down on the river.

Active slid the wriggling fish onto the beach gravel and finished it off with a rock to the head. He sliced open the red belly and tossed the guts and the vivid amber beads of its eggs into the river, then laid the carcass on Nita's rock.

"You're nearly as good as your mom with that *ulu*."

"Not as fast, though." She laid her fillets beside the new catch and eyed the harvest. "You gonna catch any more?"

He considered the matter. The two fish already landed weighed six to eight pounds apiece, he calculated, but that was before gutting and heading. Still, it was a lot of fish for four people.

"I'm thinking these'll do for tonight," he said. "And, tomorrow—well, the river is full of them." He jerked a thumb at the clear, cold water rushing downstream toward the distant Yukon.

Nita nodded and attacked the second char with her *ulu*. The slanting light traced the curve of her cheek and diminutive nose, and Active thought again how much she looked like a younger Grace.

Behind them, the setting sun glinted off the wings of the 185 beached in a little backwater behind their camp on the gravel bar. The scents of spruce and alder laced the air, mixed with wood smoke and that smell of a tumbling cold river in the last crisp moments before sunset.

Active heard the rise and fall of voices as Grace stoked what Cowboy called a bush-pilot fire: a heap of driftwood, a cup of avgas, a match, and more driftwood. Cowboy was setting up his yellow dome tent next to their blue one as she worked.

"Do you think Mom will feel better when we go berry picking tomorrow?"

"Don't know. You may have to help her a little on this trip."

Nita frowned. "Will I have to cook?"

"I hope not. We'd all be in trouble then. Maybe I'll cook."

"Yeah, right. Dads can't cook."

"This dad can."

An awkward stare froze between them. They hadn't used the word with each other before. He had been "Uncle Nathan," even after Grace adopted her and became "Mom." But now the moment had found them.

Nita turned her eyes back to her work and sliced the head off the second char. Should he say more or leave it alone?

He cleared his throat. "So, how many berries you think you'll pick tomorrow? A gallon, maybe?"

Nita stared hard at him. "Are you going to adopt me?"

So that was what was on her mind.

"I want to, but there's a legal process your mom and I have to talk about."

"Then you'd be my real dad, just like you're the baby's real dad?"

"I love you as my daughter, and that already makes me feel like I'm your real dad."

"Will you and Mom have more babies?"

"We're not sure yet."

Her face fell and she scuffed the toe of her Xtratuf in the gravel.

"But even if we have ten more, I'll still be your real dad, and you'll still be my real daughter."

She smiled to herself and went back to work with the *ulu*.

"Hey, guys, fire's ready!" Grace waved a cast-iron skillet. "Where's them fish?"

"Coming right up!" Active yelled.

He turned to Nita and winked. "Looks like no cooking for us tonight."

He put his hand up and they high-fived.

Active threw four chunks of bone-dry spruce driftwood on the campfire and watched the sparks swarm up. "Still chilly?"

"A little." Grace pulled up the hood of her *atiqluk* and took a sip of herbal tea. She gazed downriver to where a full moon was coming up through a notch in the hills. "I'm just happy we're out here."

"Me, too." He moved behind her and massaged her neck.

Cowboy stretched back in his camp chair, rubbed his belly, and dragged on a Marlboro. Nita sat on a log across from the adults, hunched over a sketch pad with a charcoal pencil.

"Can I see?" Grace asked.

Nita walked over and presented the pad. A puppy's pleading eyes looked up from the page.

"Uh-oh," Active said over Grace's shoulder.

"You said we could talk about it." Nita's eyes matched the puppy's.

Cowboy craned his neck for a peek. "You looking for a dog, sweetheart?"

Nita nodded.

"I happen to know of a dog with eyes like that—a Jack Russell terrier, I think it's called—and he needs a home."

Nita's eyes widened. "For real?"

Active grinned. "No way Nita's interested in your dog, Cowboy. She has this friend named Stacy with a puppy and he is so-o-o cute. I mean the puppy, the puppy's so-o-o cute. And if she doesn't get that puppy from him, I don't know what they'll have to talk about."

Grace slapped Active's hand and shot him a look that said, *You are so bad.*

Nita rolled her eyes. "Stacy did say his auntie might want it, so . . ."

"Lucky's pretty cute," Cowboy said.

Grace laughed and shook her head. "You have a terrier named Lucky? Why is that so hard to picture?"

"I don't exactly have him. I mean, I do, but only temporarily. He's not really mine." Cowboy flicked his Marlboro butt into the fire and gazed into the flames for a moment. "He, uh, he belonged to Evie."

Silence hung in the air like a chill. The crackling of the fire was the only sound. Nita knelt beside the pilot and gave him a hug.

"You sure you don't want him, Uncle Cowboy?"

"I do, but I'm always out flying and Linda travels all the time with her job. A dog needs his humans around."

"Evie's family doesn't want him?" Grace asked.

"No, they've got a bunch of huskies that are about half wolf."

Nita shot a look at Grace and Active. "Pleeeeeease?"

"Looks like you're on the spot here, Mom," Active said.

"Don't put this on me."

"Puppy decisions are mom stuff. Every guy knows that."

"Really? You want to go there?"

Nita stood still and looked afraid to breathe.

"Okay, let's confer." Active put his lips to Grace's ear and pretended to whisper something important. Then they looked at Nita with stone faces.

"After careful consideration," Active said, "we've decided . . ."

"Yes!" they said as one.

Nita broke into a grin. "Thank you, thank you, thank you!"

"But I'm not feeding him," Grace said in a warning tone.

"And I'm not cleaning up his poop," Active said in the same tone.

Nita ignored them. "Thank you too, Uncle Cowboy," she said. "I'll take care of Lucky just like Evie did, I promise."

Cowboy shook his head and a shadow crossed his face for a moment.

Nita glanced at Grace. "Did I say something wrong, Mom?"

"No, you didn't," Cowboy said. "I just miss her, is all."

She reached over and hugged him again.

"Thanks, kiddo."

"How about getting some sleep, sweetie?" Grace passed the sketch back to Nita. "We've got a big day of berry picking ahead of us. And I'll make some pancakes for breakfast."

Nita nodded, did a round of hugs and good nights, and headed for the tent.

The fire began to settle into its bed. The moon was high enough now to turn the river to rippling silver. Grace moved over and curled up on Active's lap. Cowboy poked at the embers with a stick.

"Hey, man, you about ready to turn in?" Active said.

"Nah, I'm gonna hang out for a while."

"Want some company?"

Cowboy sat back with a heavy sigh. "There's something about kids . . ." he said. "All that future, like money in the bank. Like Nita, all her dreams ahead of her. She gonna be a pilot, a doctor, an artist, something else we haven't even thought of?"

"Probably all of the above, knowing Nita," Grace said.

"Evie, Todd, that baby—they were probably the closest I'll ever get to any of that." The pilot fell silent and poked the fire some more. Sparks flew up again. "And then I just turned around one day and they were gone."

Something clamped onto Active's bicep. He struggled awake in the warm cocoon of the sleeping bag. Grace was pressed into his back, her nails sunk into his arm. As he pried at her hand and jerked free, she cried out and clawed at his sleeve. He rolled toward her, grasped her upper arms, and shook her.

"Wake up," he hissed. "Grace! Wake up!"

She fought him, her breath coming hard and fast. He continued to shake her gently until she relaxed and came out of it.

"Nathan." Her voice was breathy and exhausted. "Where are—"

"We're in the tent. I'm right here."

"What happ—"

"You had a dream." He stroked her between the shoulder blades. She shivered. "Your T-shirt's soaked."

He rolled it up and over her head and tossed it to the tent floor. She curled her naked torso into his chest. He rubbed her arms and shoulders until the warmth started to return.

"I was falling." She raised her head and touched his face in the dark.

He folded the sleeping bag clear of their heads. "You were falling?"

"Out of the sky. To the ground."

"In a plane?"

"It must have been. How else would I—all I remember is being really, really scared and trying to grab onto something."

"That something was my arm."

"Sorry, baby, I didn't mean to hurt you."

"I know." He cradled her against his chest and fluttered kisses down her neck.

They lay for a few minutes in silence. Active began to drift off.

Warm fingers brushed against his lower abdomen and he felt himself stirring.

"Here's something else I'd like to grab onto," she whispered.

"Even with Nita . . . ?"

"I'll be quiet."

"You?"

"I promise."

She eased on top of him and drew the sleeping bag across her shoulders as she guided him in and began a slow, silent rocking.

"You're safe now," he whispered. "Back down on planet Earth."

"Not for long." Her thighs tensed and she became wetter as they moved together. Her moment came, and when he drew her face down, she bit into his shoulder to stifle her moans.

When they were still again, he unzipped the sleeping bag and pushed the flap aside to cool them off. "Better?"

"Definitely," she murmured. Her breathing slowed as she sank toward sleep. "Hey, Nathan?"

"Yeah."

"When I was falling to the ground, when I was scared . . ."

"Yeah?"

"It wasn't for me. It was for the baby."

As the sky lightened to a feathery gray, the two men drank coffee and munched on pilot bread smeared with peanut butter. Sweet-smelling spruce smoke threaded the damp morning air.

Finally, they shouldered packs and walked past Grace and

Nita's berry buckets stacked outside the tent for the day's blueberry harvest.

The first part of the route they had scouted from the plane was easy, a cool walk through scattered spruce. But forty-five minutes in, they were bushwhacking through alders so thick Active couldn't see anything ahead except more of the python-like branches. And the mosquitoes were coming to life in the warming sun.

Over the thwack of his machete and the clank of the tools in his pack, Active heard Cowboy calling cadence a couple of yards back. "Through the jungle, sun don't shine. All I do is double time . . ."

Cowboy was playing himself in order not to think about what was over the ridge, Active supposed. The pilot came up and he played along.

"You gonna do that the whole way?"

Cowboy was a dark outline in Carhartts. Mosquitoes speckled his sleeves and swarmed his net-draped head. "Drowns out the buzzing."

"How long till we're out of this stuff?"

"Hour, maybe two. I'll break trail a while if you don't mind the wheel-dog view."

"Yeah, just let me spray myself down one more time."

They applied Deep Woods Off.

"I love the smell of DEET in the morning." Cowboy grinned.

Active didn't grin back. "You would."

Cowboy took the machete and the lead and they continued uphill. From ahead, Active heard, "Ate my breakfast too damn soon. Skeeters feast on me till noon."

Ninety minutes later, the brush thinned out with the higher elevation and they staggered on rubber legs out of the ravine and onto the rusting tundra mat that covered the gray-brown chert gravel of the upper slopes. The bugs were thinner up here, above the jungle-like vegetation that grew lower down. The two men shrugged off their packs and dropped to the ground, rolled up their head nets, and downed water and strips of dried salmon. Cowboy put on his aviators and lit a Marlboro.

Active studied the folds and peaks and streams of the Brooks Range rolling away on all sides. "God's country, huh?"

"The big empty," Cowboy said. "Wouldn't trade it for all the beaches in Hawaii."

The mountaintops across the Hawk River disappeared intermittently in the ragged clouds that sailed overhead. The higher crests showed white when the clouds parted.

Active pointed. "Think we'll get some of that?"

The pilot grunted. "Good chance, this time of year."

They passed several minutes in silence.

"Well," Cowboy said finally.

"Well," Active agreed.

They pulled on their packs and started up the slope toward the crest two hundred feet above. As they neared it, Active fell back a few yards to give Cowboy a moment with what lay on the other side.

The pilot stopped at the top, pulled off his glasses, and gazed at the scene below.

A minute or two later, Active moved up beside him. From here, up close, the ending of Evie's final flight was even more gut-wrenching than when they had passed overhead in the Navajo.

The crumpled fuselage was closest, the tail canted like a twisted cross.

The wings were perhaps a hundred yards down-slope,

apparently having sheared off as the landing gear collapsed and the fuselage plowed uphill through the tundra. The scar was still visible even now, six weeks after the crash.

Cowboy drew a deep breath. "Looks like she was moving pretty fast when she hit. You'd want that, coming down through the clouds like she was. Enough airspeed to maneuver a little, maybe set up for a survivable landing if you got some visibility at the last minute." He shook his head. "Apparently she didn't."

"You okay, buddy?" Active said. "You don't have to do this."

"I do." The pilot put his aviators back on. "You know I do."

Cowboy dropped down the slope to the fuselage. "Might as well start here, I guess," he muttered as Active caught up.

The nose of the plane rested on the tundra. The cowling lay a few feet to one side, presumably having been removed by the federal investigators. The engine had six cylinders, Active saw, laid out flat, three to a side.

Cowboy dropped his pack and peered into the engine, fished through a tangle of twisted wires and broken cables, and pulled out the end of an aluminum tube that Active took to be a fuel line.

The pilot sniffed it and shook his head. "Pretty dry, all right." He pointed at the propeller blades. "See how they're bent back? That means the engine wasn't producing power when they hit. Otherwise, the blades would have dug into the dirt and bent themselves forward."

"Like the crash report said, right?"

Cowboy grunted. "Let me pull out a couple of spark plugs."

He dug through his pack, found the right wrench, and slipped it over a spark plug on the front left cylinder. It stuck. He put his shoulders into it, heaved, grunted, heaved again, and it turned. He unscrewed it, sniffed the opening in the cylinder head, then the spark plug, and held it up between them. "Bone dry."

"It has been six weeks," Active said.

Cowboy shrugged. "An engine is sealed up pretty tight. If there was fuel in it then, there'd be some smell left even now."

He pulled out another plug with the same result and sat back on his knees.

"Hang on a minute," The pilot dug into his bag again, came up with wire cutters and another wrench, and went to work in the bowels of the engine compartment. He came up with a metal bowl.

"The fuel filter is in this thing," he said. "If there's any gas left in this airplane, it's in here."

He flipped off the cap, smelled the bowl, and turned it upside down. Nothing came out. He looked at Active and grimaced.

"Well, shit, the feds were right. Evie was completely out of fuel when she hit this mountain. But I checked those tanks myself, and so did she. They were full when she left." He looked downslope at the wings.

Active followed his gaze. "Maybe it leaked out somehow? Or the lines got plugged up?"

"Makes no sense—but what does in this mess?" Cowboy climbed to his feet and started for the wings. Halfway there, he picked up an orange ball cap from the tundra, studied it for a moment, and stuffed it into a jacket pocket.

He turned to see Active watching and shrugged.

Active nodded but didn't speak.

Cowboy started off again.

Both wings had come to rest with their tips uphill. At the other ends, severed electrical wires and silvery aluminum fuel lines dangled where the wings had separated from the fuselage. Cowboy made a circle around the left wing, then dropped to his knees at its base.

Active pulled up his jacket collar and glanced at the darkening sky. A razor-sharp wind had come up. "Looks like this stuff is moving in, all right."

The pilot ignored him and blew into a fuel line.

Over the rising wind, Active heard the pilot's breath whooshing into the line.

"If I can blow in, fuel could flow out," he muttered. He checked the line out of the other wing. It was clear, too.

"Son of a bitch." He looked up at Active. "Maybe there was a leak. Let's flip it over and look at the bottom."

Sleet pelted their heads and rattled on the wing. A raking wind gnawed at their faces. Cowboy pulled up his hood.

"I don't know about this weather," Active said. "Whatever's here, it'll still be here tomorrow. You think—"

"Go if you want. I'm staying till I figure this out."

Active took a last look at the sky and followed Cowboy to the trailing edge of the wing. They took hold and heaved. The wing rolled over and thudded onto the tundra.

They stared at the wing in disbelief, then listened again.

Active frowned. "Is that sloshing?"

"No way." The pilot pointed at one of the lines he'd just blown into. "If there was gas in this wing, it would be coming out of that line. Pouring out, in fact, because of the slope."

He grabbed the wing and rocked it on the tundra. Sloshing again. The pilot stood with hands on hips for a moment, then stuck his hand out. "Give me your pack."

Cowboy took the pack and extracted a hatchet. "One sure way

to find out." He swung the blade into the aluminum of the wing surface.

"Yeah, but . . . a metal ax on a metal fuel tank? What about sparks and . . ." Active threw out his arms to signify an explosion. "Kaboom, right?"

"I'll take my chances," Cowboy said. "Stand back."

Active retreated and tried to remember if he'd seen a fire extinguisher in the wrecked fuselage just up the hill.

Cowboy chopped away and soon had a slash a couple of feet long and two inches wide. He stuck in two fingers and felt around. "What the hell?"

"What is it?"

Without responding, the pilot went back to work with the hatchet. He extended the slash in the aluminum by another couple of feet, then chopped a perpendicular slot at each end to create a crude flap. He grabbed the edge and folded the flap back. Both men leaned forward to peer into the cavity.

Instead of avgas, they saw a white membrane bulging through the opening in the wing, undulating gently as the liquid inside sloshed back and forth.

A little of it slopped out where the hatchet or the jagged aluminum had punctured the membrane.

"What the hell!" Cowboy said again. He wet his fingers in the liquid, sniffed it, tasted it.

"Son of a bitch. This is water!"

CHAPTER FOUR

• *Monday, August 22* •

LIENHOFER AVIATION, CHUKCHI

Cowboy leaned back in a red plastic chair in the Lienhofer break room. "I still can't get my head around what we found up there."

"I know," Active said. "I've seen some strange murder weapons—a harpoon, a frying pan, even a frozen sheefish once. But giant water balloons?"

"Where do you even get something like that?"

"Internet, I'm guessing. I've got somebody on the phone to all the vendors we can Google, but needle in a haystack doesn't even begin to cover it. Meantime, those balloons might as well have come from Neptune. No company name on them, no logo, no nothing. I sent one off to the crime lab in Anchorage. They'll figure it out. Eventually. Probably. I hope."

"Only one?"

Active nodded. "I kept the other one to look at myself. For when I have an epiphany. If I have one."

Cowboy grunted absently. "Who would do that? Who *could*?"

"Somebody with not only access to your plane, but enough time to get two of those things into the tanks with no one around to interrupt." Active pulled a small leather-bound notebook from his case and set it on the table. "How would you do it, anyway? You don't just haul a big rubber bag full of water up on top of a wing and squeeze it down through the filler neck, right?"

"Hm." Cowboy walked to the big plastic aviation map on the wall and studied it in silence.

Active stood to join him. "I wish we had a less public place for this, but there's no map like this in my office."

The pilot nodded and tapped the spot where Two-Five-Mike had come to rest on the ridge above the Hawk River. He circled it with a red dry-erase marker, then put his left hand on Chukchi and his right hand on the circle.

"This is about a hundred and fifty miles," he said. "Getting there, a 207 would burn something like fourteen gallons of gas. With full tanks, you've got sixty-one gallons useable, meaning you gotta displace how much to run out where it did?"

He worked it out with the red marker on the map next to the circle:

```
  61 usbl
 -14 burned
 _____
  47 displ
```

"So," he said. "Forty-seven gallons. You'd have to displace forty-seven gallons of fuel with those bladders to leave room for your fourteen gallons in the tanks. They're gonna look full on a visual check, the gauges will say they are full, so off you go and you run out of gas an hour later. Just like Evie did."

"Take me through it," Active said. "What actually happened up there, as best as you can reconstruct it?"

"Okay, let's see. You start out on the left tank for a half hour, then switch to the right one with this selector lever on the floor between the front seats."

Halfway between Chukchi and the red circle, Cowboy drew an X. "About here, probably, is where she would have switched tanks."

Both men studied the X for a moment.

"Then you alternate every half hour," Cowboy said. "Left, right, left, right. That way, you don't end up with one wing a lot heavier than the other. Plus, you don't want to run a tank completely dry in midair if you can avoid it."

The pilot scratched his head. "Evie apparently took off with about a half hour of gas in each tank. If the left one had run dry before it came time to switch, I'm thinking she would have switched to the right one and turned back to Chukchi to get it figured out, and probably called me on the radio, too."

"So she must have switched tanks before the left one ran dry?"

"Must have, yeah," Cowboy said. "Just before, probably."

"And then—"

"And then she's on the right tank," Cowboy said. "Her gauges are telling her it's full and that the left one is three-quarters full. Everything looks totally copacetic. But a half hour later—"

"She switches back to the left tank, it runs dry, she switches back to the right tank and it runs dry too?"

Cowboy thought it over for a moment. "Something like that. One way or another, she's over the Brooks Range with a dead engine. Talk about your deafening silence."

"Been there, have you?"

The pilot grimaced. "More than once. But not like Evie, not when there was nothing under me but clouds and mountains."

"What do you make of the fact that she didn't get off a distress call?" Active said as they returned to the table. "She must have had at least a couple minutes before she was into the clouds. She was above them, right?"

Cowboy gave a rueful chuckle. "Probably not, not Evie. She had this thing she called cloud dancing. You've been on top, Nathan. You know what it's like up there in that sunlight."

"Beautiful. Like crossing the floor of heaven."

Cowboy nodded. "Cloud canyons everywhere, just like in the song. She'd drop down till she was right above the cloud deck and dance through those canyons—" The pilot's voice failed him.

Active gave him a moment, then continued. "So her engine quits, she's right on top of the clouds, so she's got almost zero time to do anything before she's in them? Is that it?"

Cowboy cleared his throat with a cough. "Yep. Total A-N-C mode. She's flying the plane on instruments, she's trying to restart the engine, she's looking for the rocks she knows are in those clouds, she's got Todd looking, and she's thinking, 'Fuck, what did I miss?' She knows nobody on the ground can help her at that point, so why waste time on the radio?"

"Yeah," Active said. "I guess not."

"And she knew her emergency beacon would go off if they went in, which it did, and people would start looking as soon as the clouds moved out, which we did."

He shook his head and fell silent, then cleared his throat again. "Anyway, where were we?"

It took Active a moment to backtrack. "We were figuring out how the guy got those bladders into the tanks."

Cowboy took a moment to refocus, then got back to his math. "So to get your forty-seven gallons of water, you'd need about twenty-three gallons in each bladder. And that would weigh—"

Cowboy paused, and this time drew numbers in the air instead of on the map.

"Wow, those bladders would weigh around two hundred pounds apiece," he said. "So, no, you wouldn't be hauling them up on top of the wings and stuffing them down the filler necks. Definitely not."

"What then?"

Cowboy rocked his chair back down. "Well, ah—"

"Well?"

The pilot slapped his forehead. "Duh. You roll up the bladder into kind of a tube, you stick it down through the filler neck into the tank, with just the mouth sticking out. Then you put in a hose and turn on the water till you've got what you need. Tie off the mouth with one of those plastic zip ties, push it down into the tank, and you're good to go."

"Don't you force fuel out and end up spilling it all over?"

"Huh." The pilot fell silent again. He pulled at his lip and took a pack of Marlboros out of his bomber jacket, tapped them on his knee, and put them away. "Not necessarily. For these short trips out to the villages and back, we usually leave with about half tanks so we can carry more of a load. When we park for the night, we're generally down to maybe quarter tanks."

"Which is—"

"About seven gallons per tank in a 207."

"Ah," Active said.

Cowboy nodded. "About what you'd want before you started filling up your bladders. So, yeah. You just put in water till the tank's full."

"Huh. When we were wrestling with the bladders up there—did it feel like there was twenty-three gallons of water in them?"

Cowboy shrugged. "Maybe. You've still got the one, right? Let's go down in the hangar and fill it up and see."

"It's back at my office," Active said. "But, yeah, later, definitely." He scrawled a reminder in his notebook.

"So, our guy," Active went on. "He had to know a lot about the Cessna 207, fuel consumption, airspeed, all of that, if he wanted to put it down where we found it, right? Are we talking about somebody here, a pilot maybe?"

Cowboy pondered for a few seconds, then shrugged.

"Not necessarily. All he really needed to know was, if he displaced a bunch of fuel with his bladders then Evie would run dry somewhere out in the country. With a little luck, somewhere she couldn't put the plane down and walk away."

"If you call that luck," Active said. "So let's talk it through. Where was your plane the night before Evie took off for Fairbanks?"

"In the hangar. Normally I keep it outside in the summer. But I pulled it inside that afternoon to change the oil."

"Who has a key to the building?"

"Anyone who works for Lienhofer's. Or ever did, probably."

Active sighed. "So other than all present and former Lienhofer employees, nobody else could have gotten into the hangar that night?"

"Ah, not exactly." Cowboy paused. "The lock on that rear door's been busted for I don't know how long. It's not like it's a fucking priority."

Active grimaced and continued. "So everyone in town had access to that hangar that night? Basically, we have about three thousand suspects?"

Cowboy shrugged. "I guess. If you count *aanas* and babies."

"Let's concentrate on the people who are normally on the premises. How many is that?"

"Sam and Delilah, the owners, of course, but they wouldn't be suspects."

"Everyone is till they're not. And?"

"We've got two pilots besides Sam and me—Sherman Stone and Pete Boskofsky. And of course Evie was one of our pilots, but . . ." He shook his head and caught a breath. "Then there's the night ramper, Jesse Apok, and the day ramper, Leon Fox. There's a janitor that comes in three, four days a week, Paul Noyakuk. And there's a new part-time girl, Dora, who does office stuff and works the ticket counter.

"So that's nine people?"

Cowboy ticked them off on his fingers and shook his head. "No, eight. Eight suspects."

Active looked at the names in his notebook and decided to get it over with. "Nine, actually."

"I miss somebody?"

"Everyone's a suspect until they're not. Anyone with motive or opportunity. Anyone who knows details about how the crime was committed. You said, 'We've got two pilots besides Sam and me.'"

"Uh-huh," Cowboy said, his voice hesitant, his expression showing he was starting to get it.

"I have to ask you questions just like I would anybody else," Active said.

"You gonna read me my rights? You wanna cuff me?"

"No, of course not. And the Miranda warning is only for people actually in custody. But I do have to ask—"

"I loved those kids like they were my own."

"I know you did. But you were maybe the last person to see them alive."

"Fuck you, Nathan."

"You wanted a police investigation. This is a police investigation."

"Well, I don't have to goddamn like it."

Active's cell phone chimed. He glanced at the screen, saw Grace's image, and sent the call to voicemail.

"Me neither, partner. One of the hardest things about being a cop. But look at it this way. I'm trying to eliminate suspects, too."

Cowboy nodded with a resentful look and stared past Active's left ear.

"We good here?" Active asked. "Or, are we going to waste time fighting over this?"

"Fuck you, Nathan. You know I'm gonna answer your questions."

"Thanks. Professionally and personally."

Cowboy nodded with a tight grin that almost looked sincere.

Active's phone pinged. "Hang on," he told Cowboy as he tapped to pull up a text from Grace.

Okay to tell Martha about the baby now, it read. *Not good if she hears it through the grapevine.*

Not good was right, Active reflected as he closed the message. But Grace had previously wanted to wait about letting his birth mother know. Now she was ready, which he took as further evidence she had made up her mind.

Plenty of raw feelings had been dug up over the years between him and Martha Active Johnson. A wild village fourteen-year-old when he was born, she had adopted him out to two white teachers at Chukchi High who'd moved to Anchorage and raised him there. The wounds had healed some over the last few years, but things were still a little touchy and, he supposed, always would be.

If she got word of her first grandchild from the river of gossip that coursed constantly through the village, well, that would be another scar they didn't need. He would have to—

Static sprayed from a circular speaker in the ceiling over the table. Then *Staying Alive* blasted down.

"What the hell is that?"

"Delilah's experiment with piped-in music!" Cowboy yelled as the Bee Gees keened on. "The system only works every couple days, and then it just goes off at random like that."

"Can we turn it off?"

"No!" Cowboy shouted. "Just give it a couple of minutes! It'll go off by its—"

The music died.

CHAPTER FIVE

• *Monday, August 22* •

LIENHOFER AVIATION, CHUKCHI

Active was looking over his notes, waiting for his ears to stop ring-ing, when a curvy twenty-something with caramel skin and a lush crown of loose black curls entered the breakroom and strode to the soda machine near the door. Half black and half Inupiat, he guessed. He didn't recall ever having seen her around town.

He slapped his notebook shut, caught Cowboy's eye, and jerked his head at the map. Cowboy processed for a moment, then went over and erased his work.

The newcomer put a couple of bills into the machine as she swayed in her purple anorak to whatever was coming through her headphones. After several seconds with no soda, she hammered the front of the pop machine with her fists.

"You have to kick it down there at the bottom right corner," Cowboy called across the room. "See where the dents are? Then push your foot against it and rock it back."

Headphone Girl continued to batter the machine. "Oh, you gonna snatch my money, bitch? Is that how it is? You gonna take my last dollar?"

Cowboy cupped his hands over his ears and pointed at Headphone Girl. "I'll be right back." He crossed the room and delivered a kick that coaxed a Diet Pepsi from the machine. Headphone Girl flashed him a bright smile, retrieved her soda from its compartment, and strode out of the room. Cowboy returned to his seat.

"Who was that?" Active asked.

"That's Monique."

"She wasn't on your list. Does she work here?"

"Close by. She's Dora's cousin. I met her this morning when they were hanging out at the ticket counter. She's with the Weather Service."

Active added "Monique" to the list of suspects, then flipped to a new page in his notebook. "Okay, so, anybody have a beef with Evie or Todd?"

Cowboy frowned in thought as he drew the Marlboro pack out again. He fished inside with an index finger, snagged a lone, broken cigarette, then crumpled it and the pack and tossed them on the table. "Not at Lienhofer's. Everybody liked Evie. And Todd? Shoot, I think even Delilah was sweet on him." His lip curled into a half smile. "Never saw the dragon lady act that human with anybody else."

"What about around Chukchi? *Naluaqmiu* doctor rides into town, sweeps a cute little village girl off her feet. That get anybody bent out of shape?"

"Sure, Todd was all that, but he never played the great white father or anything. He'd set a kid's broken arm or diagnose an old lady's bladder infection, then be shooting hoops with the guys at the gym a half hour later."

"He ever talk about getting crossways with anyone?"

"Not up here. But he was engaged to this girl from a family of one-percenters back in Houston. She was Miss Texas, her mother's old oil money, her dad's a world-famous plastic surgeon known as the King of Cleavage. The fiancée's plan was, Todd would join Dad's practice and they'd be the town's golden couple."

"And instead he runs off to be a bush doctor in Alaska."

"Oh, yeah. Their engagement was apparently the talk of Texas. It was a capital-E Event when he called it off. She sent him some nasty emails, said he'd regret it someday."

"Like death threats? Was she serious?"

Cowboy shrugged. "Who knows? How do you tell with a woman?"

"I'm not sure they're ever not serious."

"Seems like it," Cowboy said. "Hell hath no fury and all that. But a Texas beauty queen sneaking up here and sabotaging a bush plane?"

"She has money. She could have hired someone."

Cowboy shot him a skeptical look.

"Yeah," Active said. "It is pretty far-fetched. What about Evie's family, they like him?"

"Her brothers weren't too wild about him at first. Their attitude was, what does a guy like him see in a village girl? Is it for real, or is she just there to pass time till he gets back on the jet one day?"

Active nodded. "Those Kavoonah boys are a pretty rough bunch, all right. I think I've hauled 'em all in at one time or another. Standard knucklehead stuff—assault, disorderly conduct."

"Yeah, but only with each other. I never knew one of 'em to hurt anybody else."

Active took a minute to scroll back through his encounters with the Kavoonah brothers. "You're right about that."

"Five boys, three fathers, none still involved," Cowboy said. "You can see where they might some have issues with life. They had different last names, but the kids all used Kavoonah, their mom's second husband's name. Anyway, Todd won 'em over pretty quick. He was like that. Impossible to hate."

"What about Evie's father?"

"She and the youngest brother shared him. He died when his snowgo went through the ice back on the lagoon. She was around five at the time, shy little girl. She needed a father figure, and somehow that turned out to be me. I was happy to do it, since Linda and I can't have any of our own." He seemed to vanish inside himself for a moment, then grunted. "Anyway, Evie was looking for a way to get out of her own family, was how I saw it. That's why she became a pilot, and I was glad to help her with that, too. Our plan was, she was gonna be the first Eskimo girl in the captain's seat of an Alaska Airlines jet."

"How did she meet Todd?"

"A couple of the brothers got in a fight. One ended up with a dislocated jaw, the other one had a cracked rib. Evie drove them to the emergency room."

"Wait a minute," Active said. "Why don't I remember that?"

"Probably kept it in the family," Cowboy said. "Why wouldn't they, if they had records already?"

Active nodded.

"So anyway," Cowboy went on, "Dr. Todd Brenner just happens to be on duty when this cute little honey with blazing black eyes and an orange ball cap drags in these two busted-up morons."

"Love at first sight, was it?"

"First fight, more like. They're still throwing punches while she's trying to keep them apart and, by golly, she's holding her own. Todd comes in, calms 'em down, patches 'em up, then takes her out for coffee and the hospital cafeteria's world-famous lemon meringue pie. The rest, as they say, is history."

"What about you and him? You two ever get into it, maybe him not treating her right?"

Cowboy glared. "We got along great. He treated her like a queen. And, remember, that was supposed to be me in the plane with him, not Evie. If I wanted to take him out, what fucking sense does it make that I would go along for the ride?"

"Who knew it was supposed to be you?"

"It was on the schedule, so, pretty much everyone at Lien-hofer's. Plus the guys at the shop in Fairbanks where I was going to pick up the radios. And I was going to get a crown redone while I was over there, so my dentist, his office people. Oh, and Linda ordered some quilting supplies from one of the shops and wanted me to pick those up to save on the shipping costs. She gave them a heads-up, so the quilt lady knew—and Linda, of course, and whoever she told, they all knew I was coming. Also whoever Todd might have told?"

"That's a lot of folks. Anyone have a beef with you?"

Cowboy buried his face in his hands for a few seconds. "I guess I rub people the wrong way once in a while, but nothing to make anybody want to kill me." He shook his head. "That I know of, anyway."

"How exactly did Evie end up in that plane instead of you?"

Cowboy sank lower in his chair.

"Like I said before, I was taking it to Fairbanks for the new radios. Todd asked if he could ride along and get in some cross-country time for his pilot's license. He was thinking maybe they'd get their own plane someday."

"But instead of you, Evie went."

"She called me the night before, about ten o'clock."

"At Lienhofer's?"

"No, I was at the E-Z Market getting some smokes and onion rings."

"And all of a sudden she wants to take your plane?"

"Yeah," the pilot said. "She and Todd were talking about the baby, and I guess things started getting all gushy and he popped the question. Out of the blue. Now, she said, Todd wanted them to fly to Fairbanks to buy an engagement ring. And she had that doctor's appointment out there the day after. How could I say no? She was so excited, she could barely talk. You know how kids are."

"So let's see. The tanks were a quarter full when you pulled it into the hangar that afternoon, right? And somebody filled them up for you?"

"Would have been Jesse Apok, the night ramper I told you about. I put it on the schedule and Two-Five-Mike was out on the tarmac the next morning with full tanks, just like I asked." Cowboy paused and shook his head. "They looked full, anyway."

"What time does Jesse get off?"

"Whenever the last flight of the day gets in and he puts the plane to bed. In the summer, maybe ten o'clock, midnight."

Cowboy's cell rang, and he held up a forefinger to Active as he barked "yeah" twice into the phone and hung up. "Looks like I gotta go to Tanana." He looked at his watch. "Can we wrap this up?"

"Yeah, almost done. You didn't go back that night at all?"

"No, dammit. What's with the third degree? If I was your killer, would I twist your arm to go up there and investigate the fucking crash?"

Active chewed his lip for a moment. "Look, if you were here that night, you might have seen the killer without knowing it."

The pilot shook his head. "But I didn't, because I wasn't here."

Active kept his voice level. "It's important to establish a timeline, so let's just gut this out, okay? What time did you see them that morning?"

"I met them here around six. No one else was around yet. When I walked up on them, they were in a pretty serious lip lock."

"And then?"

"Like I told you before, I checked the tanks. They were full. Evie did a walk-around and she checked them, too. She gave me a big hug and climbed in and off they went."

Cowboy turned away and gazed out the window overlooking the tarmac. Active waited in silence until the pilot cleared his throat and turned back.

"What about them? Any problems in the relationship? The baby, maybe?"

Cowboy rubbed his jaw and shifted in his chair. "Well, it wasn't actually planned. Evie wasn't even sure she wanted kids. She was too freaked out about her own family, you know?"

The overhead speaker sputtered again, and Neil Diamond serenaded them with "Sweet Caroline" for a half minute before going silent. Cowboy rolled his eyes. "That's so fucking annoy—"

A female voice begged "Help Me Make it Through the Night" for twenty seconds, then faded out.

Neither man spoke for a moment as they awaited another ambush from the rogue speaker.

"Delilah could at least update her playlist," Active said.

"Reliving her youth," Cowboy said.

"All right. So the brothers didn't quite trust Todd, at least for a while. Here she had found someone who made her happy, and they were being the same old knuckleheads. That must've been hard on her."

"Yeah, but the Kavoonah boys came around eventually. Evie and Todd were really in love. It was like the sun came out whenever they walked into a room. Kind of swept you up when you saw it."

"But she had a lot on her mind, right? Like her brothers might still find some way to screw things up, or she might miscarry? Was there any real hint something was about to happen that morning? I mean, that hug she gave you?"

"Like she killed herself and Todd because she was scared about the pregnancy or because of a little family friction? Come on, Nathan."

"I hear you. But you have to start a thing like this by not ruling anything out, not even the crazy stuff. Tunnel vision has been the ruin of many an investigation."

"I guess," Cowboy said. "But this is one possibility I am personally ruling out. And not discussing anymore. Evie did not put those balloons in the fuel tanks."

"Got it." Active pushed back his chair and stood up. "I think it's time for a talk with Jesse Apok." He dropped the notebook into his case and glanced across Chukchi's main east-west runway as he walked past the window. A flicker of motion near a cluster of buildings at the near end of the graveled north-south strip caught his eye. He moved closer to the glass for a better look. "Hey, Cowboy. Come over here."

The pilot walked up beside him. "What?"

"That," Active pointed. "What is that?"

Cowboy's gaze followed Active's extended finger. His eyes widened and he pushed his hat back.

"Son of a bitch."

CHAPTER SIX

• Monday, August 22 •

WEATHER STATION, CHUKCHI

The white globe separated from the outstretched arm of the figure in the purple anorak and drifted upward.

"A weather balloon." Cowboy slapped the break room window. "Of course. I've seen them launched over there a hundred times. It just didn't register when we pulled them out of Two-Five-Mike up on that ridge."

Two minutes later, Active stopped the Tahoe at a low green building near the north end of the gravel strip with its line of tiny Pipers and Cessnas tied down along the side. He looked up as he stepped out of the Chevy. The weather balloon was a mere speck now in the pale blue sky.

He bounded up the building's four wooden steps. A sign on the wall read, NATIONAL WEATHER SERVICE, CHUKCHI, ALASKA, BLDG. 101. Hinges creaked as he pushed into a rush of warm air.

"Be with you in a minute." Monique sat at a counter facing

three computer monitors, with her back and her halo of curls to the door. Light poured in through big, half-shaded windows behind the counter. Tiny yellow tundra flowers peeked from a Diet Pepsi can on the sill. Next to it stood a framed photo obscured by the glare off the picture glass.

"Coffee's over there." A slender arm pointed at the wall to her left. She leaned into the screen and tapped the keyboard.

Active's eyes roamed the map-covered walls, the collection of printers and modems spread out on the counter, papers with columns of numbers push-pinned to bulletin boards, and a half-dozen clipboards racked in the slots of a metal desk organizer. Beside the counter, the purple anorak was draped across the front paws of a four-foot-high black bear chainsawed from a log.

He found a clean black coffee mug with pink polka dots next to the half-full coffee pot and poured himself a cup, then took a sip. "Not bad for government coffee," he said.

"My coffee." She swiveled around to face him. "One hundred percent Arabica from Tanzania. I get it from Amazon once a month." Her smile gleamed in her dark-honey face.

He smiled back. "Monique, right?"

"Monique Rogers," she said with a hint of puzzled frown. "Do I—oh yeah, you were at Lienhofer's with that pilot earlier."

He extended his hand. "Nathan Active, Chief of Public Safety for the borough."

She gave his hand a quick squeeze and waved him into an office chair on wheels. "How can I help you?" The computer screen behind her glowed with charts and colored bars and circles. "You're a cop? Some kind of security situation going on?"

"No, nothing like that." Active leaned back and rested the mug on his knee. "I saw the weather balloon go up and got curious about how all that works."

Monique relaxed and her smile returned.

"You the only one who does it?" he asked.

"That's me. Twice a day—three P.M., three A.M."

He leaned around her to look at the monitors. "So what does that balloon tell you?"

She swiveled and picked up a small, white box with an antenna and a couple of other appendages poking out. "This is a radiosonde. I tie it on with a string, send up the balloon, and it tells us temperature, relative humidity, wind speed, and wind direction as the balloon goes up. We use the data to make our forecasts."

She waved at the equipment on the counter like a game show hostess. "I check here to see if it's transmitting. That lasts maybe an hour and a half before the balloon explodes about a hundred thousand feet up, and the radiosonde falls back to earth."

She pointed at a glowing green bullseye crossed with a squiggle on the computer screen.

Active rolled in closer.

"This wiggly line here is the trajectory of the balloon I just launched. It's tracking northeast about thirty degrees, around ten thousand feet up now."

Active nodded with feigned comprehension. "I see. So, you work twelve hours a day?"

She added a laugh to the smile. "I work a split shift. I take care of the data, take off, then come back in for the second launch. I'm two weeks on, two off, except in July when my alternate was on vacation for a month. Then I was a one-woman show."

"How do you fill up the balloons?"

"I'll show you." She stood up, grabbed the anorak off the

chainsawed bear, and led him outside. They walked past a purple Jeep Wrangler parked beside the office to a turquoise, two-story building with a double garage door that faced the gravel strip. Monique pulled out a key ring and let them in through a side door.

In the center of the cavernous room was a big metal table. At one end stood a cylindrical tank with nozzles and gauges on top. "Is that helium?"

"Hydrogen," Monique said. "It's cheaper."

"Where are the balloons?"

Monique walked to a tall metal cabinet and opened one of the double doors. "In here."

Four deep shelves were stacked with dozens of wrinkled, white cocoons. "That's a lot of balloons."

"About two hundred of these little guys. The weather service ships them up in bulk." She tapped an invoice on a clipboard that hung on the inside of the cabinet door. "Latex balloon, 100 count," was typed near the top of the pink sheet of paper. "I go through a lot of 'em. Two a day, every day."

Active leaned into the cabinet for a closer look. "Do you count them every day?"

"No need, I go by the date of the last shipment on the invoice, so I'll know when to reorder."

"So, if a couple disappeared, you wouldn't necessarily know?"

She shot him a puzzled look. "Disappeared? How? I keep the building locked. Last thing we need is having some drunk stumble in and get into the hydrogen, right?"

"You're the only one with a key?"

"The only one on site. My supervisor has a key, but he flies in from Fairbanks maybe three times a year." The puzzled frown came back. "Is this an investigation? Should I call my supervisor?

If you're looking for information, he's probably who you should be talking to."

"No need. Really, I'm just curious how things work." Active walked over to the metal table. "Is this where you fill up the balloons?"

"Yes." Her face softened, and she seemed to relax a bit. "Would you like to see one?"

"Sure."

She pulled a balloon from the cabinet, unfolded it, and laid it out on the table.

It stretched about thirty inches from the mouth to the top and about twenty inches across the middle, Active estimated. Just like the balloons from Two-Five-Mike.

"Doesn't look like it's very scientific, does it?" she said. "It takes about six minutes to inflate, but I can't do it now because I don't have another launch for about eleven hours. I have to be exact so the data is transmitted at the right time. Hundreds of weather balloons all around the world go up at the same time every day."

Active ran his hand over the cool, rubbery surface. Not bulky, easy to manipulate, easy to stuff down the neck of a fuel tank. "How big does it get when you inflate it?"

"About six feet in diameter. It expands to about forty feet in the atmosphere, then it explodes."

"How do you get it outside?"

"Very carefully. First, I tie on the radiosonde and tether the balloon to the table here." She pointed at an iron loop at the end of the table. She walked to the garage door and pushed a button. The door groaned upward. "Then I untether the balloon and run like hell to get clear of the building before the wind catches it."

Monique took off in a sprint and Active chased after her. She stopped a hundred feet out on the gravel apron. The wind whipped her hair into a chocolate cloud. "I check my watch." She raised her left wrist as she spoke, then lifted her right arm and face to the sky. "And I let it fly."

Active's eyes followed the imaginary balloon.

"So, Chief Active, have I satisfied your curiosity?"

"Pretty much, but I'd like another cup of that coffee, if you don't mind."

Back inside, Active sipped from the pink-and-black mug as Monique checked off items on a clipboard. "How long have you had this job?"

"Almost nine months. My contract is up September twenty-third. I finish this rotation Friday, then I'm off for my two, then one more stretch and I'm done. It's a long way from being a TV weather girl in California, but I wanted to try something different."

"Mission accomplished, I'd say. How do you like Chukchi?"

"Believe it or not, I lived up here with my folks when I was a baby. This is my mom's village. She met my dad when she lived in Fairbanks and he was stationed at the Army base there. And my cousin Dora still lives up here. So Chukchi's home. Or home-ish, anyway."

"Spend much time at Lienhofer's?"

"No. Actually, I was never up there before today, and that was only because Dora just got hired there and I was checking in with her. Basically, I just do my work, hop in my Jeep, go home, listen to my music, and chill."

"Doesn't sound like much of a life for a single gal."

"A drama-free break on the edge of nowhere can be a good thing sometimes."

Active shielded the photo on the sill behind her to cut the glare and took a close look. A small, white dog, ears cocked. He tipped his head toward the image. "Cute little guy there. That brown patch around the one eye makes him look like he's winking."

"Too cute for his own good, all right. He totally works it."

"What kind of dog is that?"

"A Jack Russell terrier. Or terrorist, as some people call 'em. They're lovable, but they're kind of high-energy."

"I'll bet he's great company."

Monique glanced backward and smiled. "Used to be. I don't have him anymore."

"No?"

"I work weird hours. I thought he'd be better off with someone else, so I found him a new home."

"Huh. I know a pilot who gave a dog away because of his weird hours, too. You ever make friends with any of the Lienhofer pilots?"

"Don't know any of them. Except the guy I met today, the one with you. Cowboy, right?"

"Cowboy Decker. Nobody else?"

Her eyes flicked left for a second, which usually meant a witness was cooking up a story. Honest reflection was generally signified by eyes right.

"Well," she began. "Yes, I did meet that girl pilot one time. The one that died in the plane crash?"

"Evie Kavoonah?"

"Yeah, that's her. Pretty girl." She rolled her eyes. "In a plain kind of way."

"Met her at Lienhofer's, did you?"

"No. Like I said, I was never there before today. It must've been somewhere else around town, I forget where."

"Uh-huh." Active waited her out.

Finally, Monique said, "That was terrible, how she died."

"And her fiancé, too."

Monique fiddled with the clipboard. She uncrossed and recrossed her legs. "Yeah. What a shame. They probably burned up, right?"

"Killed on impact. Were you working the night before it happened?"

She looked up and seemed to have trouble steadying her gaze. "Yeah, I guess I was. Probably. I mean, I'm normally here from two to four A.M. to do the launch and make sure the data's transmitting. I don't know why I wouldn't have been."

Active looked at Monique's lime and turquoise Nike sneakers and another pair, green and purple, at the end of the counter. "You run?"

"Oh, yeah, religiously. Every day. A sound mind in a sound body. My dad drilled that into me. My only vice is Diet Pepsi, one a week max."

"You ever run out around the airport?"

"Sure. A lot of times in the middle of the night. Especially in summer. It's so peaceful, that weird gray twilight you get up here. Ghost light, I call it."

"Up by Lienhofer's, maybe?"

"Uh-huh, sometimes I'll loop up to the Lienhofer hangar there, catch my breath, head back."

"How about the night before Evie took that plane up?"

"Not sure. Probably. That was, what, a couple months ago?"

"About six weeks, actually."

She tilted her head and narrowed her eyes. "You know, Chief Active, I think you *are* investigating something. Was that crash maybe not an accident like they said on Kay-Chuck?"

"Any reason to think otherwise?"

"What would I know about it?"

"Sometimes a person will see something that turns out to be important later without realizing it at the time. Like that night, you're taking your run around the tarmac, there's a gentle breeze blowing, that warm east wind we get off the tundra in the summer, the moon is out. It's so peaceful and quiet, that ghost light like you say. But then, maybe there's somebody around, something going on you didn't expect to see. Nothing major, but maybe it registers subconsciously."

"Who? Where?"

"Maybe around the hangar, while you stop to catch your breath? Maybe you hear something? Maybe you go inside the hangar to check it out?"

"No. I told you, I was never in that hangar."

"Right," Active said. "Why would you be?"

"Anyway, they must lock it, right? How would I get in?"

"Exactly. How would you?" He braced his hands on his knees, stood up, and returned the mug to its place. "Thanks for the coffee."

"Good luck with your investigation, Chief."

He glanced at his watch as he stepped out of the weather station. Two hours till Jesse Apok was due on shift at Lienhofer's. Just enough time to go by E-Z Market for the dog food Nita wanted for Lucky, drop by Martha's office at the school administration building, and pick up Danny Kavik at Public Safety before swinging by Apok's place.

He could brief Kavik on the balloons in the 207's tanks and the long roster of potential suspects on the ride over. It was time for Chukchi Public Safety's newest officer to graduate from de-escalating fistfights and tracking down stolen snowgos and get his feet wet in a homicide investigation.

Active opened the weather station door, then paused and glanced back at Monique. "That dog. What's his name?"

"Hercules."

"Huh. Big name for a little dog."

"Yep. But he totally owns it."

CHAPTER SEVEN

• *Monday, August 22* •

SCHOOL DISTRICT ADMINISTRATION BUILDING, CHUKCHI

Martha sat behind her desk, brow furrowed, and squinted at a sheet of paper on her blotter. Active stood in the office doorway, unobserved by the director of the Chukchi Borough School District's teacher-aide program. She held the paper up to catch the light from a window behind her.

"*Arii,* why they print this so small? How they expect—"

"*Aaka?*"

Martha's face lit up with that sunrise of a smile as she turned her dark, sparkling eyes on him. "Nathan, what a nice surprise! Nothing but bad news all day, the budget, staff cuts, but now my baby comes to see his mother!"

She stood and threw out her arms and he crossed the room for a hug.

"Well, I have some news that will—"

A polite knock sounded behind them.

"Martha?" A young Inupiat woman stood in the doorway with a manila folder. "I'm sorry to interrupt. Do you have time to sign this stuff before you go?"

Martha beckoned her in. "*Arii*, Jocelyn, I forget I'm leaving early today."

Jocelyn laid the folder on the desk and eyed Active shyly while Martha signed the paperwork. Active nodded as the assistant gathered up the documents and left.

"You're leaving early?" Active asked.

She raised her brows in the Inupiat yes. "I have an appointment with the eye doctor." She grimaced. "Time for glasses, maybe. Your *aaka*'s not so young anymore."

"Oh, you're as beautiful as ever."

She beamed again and gave him a dismissive wave, but it wasn't false praise. She was in sight of fifty, but her skin still glowed, wrinkle-free except for the feathery lines around her mouth and eyes. Only a few strands of white streaked the shoulder-length black hair. And, of course, there was that dazzling smile, which seemed unmarked by the passage of time.

She grabbed a jacket from the back of her chair. Active helped her slip it on.

"You got a minute for my news before you go?" he asked. He was usually the one too busy to visit, while Martha was forever coaxing him to stay an extra hour or two at her house with the promise of moose stew or with a guilt-trip plea that his half brother, Sonny, was due home soon and would be crushed to miss him.

"I was going to walk to the clinic, so I have to go pretty soon, all right?"

"I could drive you."

Her face lit up and she settled back into her chair. "*Arigaa*, we have a few minutes, then. What's your news?"

Active perched on a corner of the desk. He had rehearsed the big announcement. He would play games with her a little, hint around until she almost guessed, then unwrap the package. But now, as he looked down at her unsuspecting expression, an uncontrollable grin spread across his face. The words burst from his mouth of their own accord.

"We're having a baby."

She leapt up and threw her arms around him, and he almost fell off the desk. He stood up to regain his balance as she held his hands and danced from side to side and sang, "I'm gonna be an *aana*! I'm gonna be an *aana*!"

The commotion drew a little crowd to the door. Applause and cries of "*Yoi!*" and "*Arigaa!*" broke out. Finally, she let him go and collapsed back into her chair. The cheering section waved and drifted away.

Martha, grinning and teary, shook a finger at him. "Your *aaka* is always right, ah? Didn't I say, you should stay in Chukchi with Gracie, not move to Anchorage like you always talk about? Now you gonna be a daddy and I'm gonna be an *aana*! How soon? How is Gracie? No problems?"

"The ultrasound shows she's about fourteen weeks along, so that would be, uh—" He couldn't remember the due date that Grace had given him. Were only men so bad at details like this?

"And I was right about the *quiyuk* too, ah?" She caught his expression. "I'm sorry, I know you always tell me, don't ask about if you and Gracie are—"

"And I'm still telling you."

"How else was I gonna be an *aana* if you two weren't—"

"*Aaka*."

"*Arii*, sorry, sorry. At least everything's good now. Not like when I had you and—"

"*Aaka*, we don't have to go there every time."

Martha's face collapsed and she began to sob.

"*Aaka*, come on. It's all good now, like you said."

"Ah, my baby. Sometimes I always think this will never happen. You'll never find someone good for you—maybe you'll stay with that Lucy Generous. I know she's nice girl, all right, but I never think she's right one for you."

Active realized with a spasm of terror that one more awkward conversation about the baby lay ahead. Lucy Generous Brophy was married now, with two kids of her own, but she made it no secret that her heart's eye still gazed down the road they might have traveled together if Grace Palmer had not come along.

Now she was the office manager at Chukchi Public Safety, her office right next to his. The conversation could not be avoided. The question was, would he get there before the news did?

He wrenched himself back to Martha's teary monologue.

"I think maybe I mess you up," she was saying, "the way you start out. Maybe you'll never have a family of your own."

He took her hand and gave it a squeeze. "But now I do. And you're part of it. Every baby needs its *aana*."

Martha pulled her hand free and stroked the back of his hand. "I see Gracie only couple days ago, she never say nothing."

"She wasn't ready to talk about it yet."

"Oh, that poor girl, she have a hard time from all what she go through. You be careful with her, Nathan. Don't stress her out, so that baby will come out right."

"I'm trying, *aaka*. But sometimes it's like tiptoeing across black ice. One wrong step and—crack!—you go through."

"We're like that when we're having a baby," she said. "Hormones, what they call it now. Early days ago, we Inupiat just call it, we're having a baby."

He sighed. "Didn't the old-timers make pregnant women go off by themselves to have their babies? I'm thinking that still might not be a bad idea today. For everyone involved."

She grinned. "Now you really talk like a man got no clue. But maybe Gracie should see that Nelda Qivits again, ah?"

Active nodded. "I think she's leaning that way, all right."

Martha folded her arms, and her face took on a glow of satisfaction. "Wait until I tell Leroy he's gonna be an *attata*. He'll be so happy, another kid he can teach to hunt and fish like Nita and Sonny."

"What about me?" Active feigned a look of hurt. "You don't think I could teach—"

"Naw, Leroy's way better. Better than most Eskimos."

They both laughed. Leroy Johnson, Martha's husband and Sonny's father, had not a single strand of Inupiat DNA in his genes. But turn him loose in the country, and nobody would bring home more meat.

"Have you told the Wilhites?" Martha's voice was hesitant. The Wilhites were Active's adoptive parents, another subject perpetually on the touchy list in their conversations.

"No, not yet," he said, and added, "We wanted you to know first."

She smiled with pleasure, but politely turned her head away to hide it.

"What about Sonny? You think he'll be excited to be an uncle?"

"Yeah, I'll tell him soon as he gets home from school." She paused. "Unless you want—"

"No, you go ahead. I'll catch him later." Active had a hard time keeping up with his half brother. Sonny was a senior in high school now, a computer whiz, and already deep into basketball practice for the coming season. And, judging from what Active saw online, juggling a girl or two interested in being more than just Facebook friends.

"You better watch that Sonny," Martha said. "He'll have your little one dribbling a basketball soon as he's walking."

"Or 'she,'" Active said. "I hear Grace was pretty good on the court back in the day."

Martha raised her eyebrows in acknowledgment, then glanced at the clock on the wall behind Active. "I guess we better get going."

"Need some help, grandma?" He offered his hand.

She slapped it away and stood up. "Don't you worry about me. I'll never be too old to spoil my grandbaby rotten."

As they stepped outside, a gust of wind kicked up dust from the gravel parking lot. He opened the Tahoe's passenger door and helped her in.

She touched his hand and looked at him. "I'm so proud of you, Nathan."

"Thanks, *aaka*. I guess we're all gonna make it, ah?"

CHAPTER EIGHT

• *Monday, August 22* •

DEPARTMENT OF PUBLIC SAFETY, CHUKCHI

Jesse Apok sat in a metal folding chair, arms crossed over a narrow chest and a scowl slashed across his face. "What's this about, man? *Arii,* you gonna make me late for work. I'll get fired."

Active sat across from Apok at a fake wood-grain table in the windowless cave of the interrogation room.

Danny Kavik leaned against a corner a few feet away. "The sooner you cooperate and answer a few questions, the sooner you're on your way," he said in a friendly voice.

Apok had required a bit of persuasion to ride with the officers from his place to the Public Safety Building. Kavik had put him at ease with a couple of jokes about Apok's jump shot when they played together years before on the basketball team at Chukchi High.

Active recalled his first conversation with Danny Kavik. Active had been working on a murder case; the kid was a security guard at the Gray Wolf mine in the mountains north of Chukchi. Danny had asked about openings on the Chukchi police force so that he could stay close to home and take care of his ailing mother and four younger siblings. His ambition and intellect had been apparent.

He'd left Kavik in charge during the trip with Cowboy to the Hawk River. That hadn't sat well with Alan Long, who had several years on the force, but sometimes you had to go with savvy over seniority.

"What do you want to know?" Apok shifted his gaze from Kavik to Active.

"You've been at Lienhofer's for a while, right?" Active scraped his chair forward a couple of inches and rested his forearms on the table on either side of his notebook.

"Yeah, I've been a ramper there for almost two years."

"Always on the night shift?"

"Yeah. Six to midnight, sometimes later if there's a late flight coming in." He uncrossed his arms, stroked his sparse mustache with a thumb, and glanced at Kavik. "Can I smoke in here?"

The younger officer nodded at a NO SMOKING sign on the wall.

"*Arii.*" Apok ran his hand over the back of his head, where his stringy black hair was fastened into a foot-long ponytail.

"Full-time?" Active asked.

"Yeah. Monday through Saturday."

"That doesn't leave much time for a girlfriend, does it?"

Apok shrugged. "No girlfriend. Only an ex-girlfriend, and she's got the kid. Three years old and I don't hardly ever get to see him."

"But I bet you've got child support, ah?" Kavik said, scooping up the ball like a point guard. "Can't afford to take time off, right?"

"You got that right, man." Apok grimaced and propped his elbows on the table.

Kavik pulled out a chair, reversed it, and straddled it. With his smooth face and close-cropped hair, he looked like he'd still fit in at Chukchi High. "Not even a couple of days to catch some caribou up the Katonak? You and Paul Noyakuk used to take the boat out every year, ah?"

The ramper squinted and wrinkled his nose in the Inupiat no.

"No time for caribou hunting now?" Kavik asked.

Apok's eyes bounced around the room. "Nah, just work. Like you said, I gotta pay that child support, all right. Hey, could I get a Coke or something?"

Kavik pushed up from his chair.

"In a minute," Active said. "So, Jesse. You were working the night before that plane crash last month? Cowboy Decker's 207?"

Apok jerked upright and glanced at Kavik. "Yeah, I was at work. All night. I didn't even take off for dinner."

"And why do you remember that?" Active asked.

The ramper shrugged.

"No dinner, huh? That happen a lot, you work your whole shift without a break?"

"Nah, I keep track of my time off, that's all."

"Why's that?" Kavik asked. "You ever take too long for dinner? Maybe catch hell from the boss?"

"No . . . well, yeah, maybe a couple of times. Wasn't no big deal. Delilah wouldn't never have known if that Cowboy never bitch about it. He almost get me fired, all right."

"That piss you off?" Kavik asked. "*Naluaqmiu* messing with your paycheck like that? You ever want to get even?"

"It pissed me off. But I got over it. You know, like when we played ball, coach would say, 'Shake it off,' and we'd keep playing?"

"So you didn't take a long dinner break that night?" Active continued.

"Nah, like I said, no dinner. Cowboy wanted that plane fueled up and ready to go in the morning. If somebody fucked up, it wasn't me. It was that Evie. That announcer say on Kay-Chuck it was pilot error, fuel exhaus—" The ramper's mouth slammed shut and his eyes rabbited around the room.

"I'll get that Coke." Kavik rose and stepped out.

Active drummed his fingers on the table and stared down at his notes. He let the silence stretch on, watching Apok's discomfort build. The ramper checked the watch on his bony wrist. His foot began a rhythmic tap-tap-tap.

"Yeah, Jesse, she ran out of gas, that's what the government report said. How would that happen, if you filled up the tanks?"

Apok pulled a phone out of his jacket and stared at the screen. Active slapped a palm on the table. The ramper jolted back to attention.

"I said, how could she run out of gas if you filled up the tanks?"

"Maybe there was a leak," Apok said. "All I know is, I filled it up. It was ready to go, just like Cowboy said."

"Notice anything unusual with the tanks, the pump, how much fuel it took to fill up, any sign of a leak, anything?"

"No, same as always, everything was the same as always."

"Were those tanks empty before you filled them up?"

"No—actually, yeah—" Apok's brow furrowed in concentration. Finally he said, "I don't remember exactly." He hung his head for a moment and stared at the table as if he might find the answers to Active's questions there. "They're usually pretty low when the pilots finish for the day, but not empty. Anyway, what does that have to do with me? The pilots are supposed to check that shit before they take off. Maybe Evie didn't do that. You know, like the report said. Pilot error."

"You knew Evie Kavoonah was going to take that plane up the next morning?"

"No. I only found out she was the pilot when I heard about the crash. Last thing I knew was, Cowboy was gonna fly it and he told me to fuel it up and that's what I did."

Active clicked his ballpoint a few times and made a note in his notebook. "How much fuel did those tanks take?"

Apok shifted in his chair and rolled his shoulders. His foot tapped faster. "Whatever they take. They can take sixty-one gallons if they're all the way empty."

Active scrawled again in his notebook. "That's how much fuel you put in? Sixty-one gallons?"

"No, maybe about forty-five or so, probably."

Kavik came in, set a Coke in front of Apok, and resumed his seat.

Apok took a long, loud swig of soda. "I mean, they don't run them all the way empty. But we don't log how much we put in." He looked at the younger officer and his eyes pleaded. "Danny, you don't think I had nothing to do with that girl getting killed, ah? *Arii*, man, I never."

"Did you know Todd Brenner?" Active asked.

"The doc that was killed too? Sure, I seen him around. He was taking lessons from Cowboy. He seemed like an okay guy."

"What about Evie?"

"I knew her a little, just enough to say hi. Everybody knew Evie Kavoonah. She was nice."

"Ever say anything more than just 'hi'?"

"Yeah, I guess so. I'd text her a happy face sometimes."

"You texted her? That happen a lot?"

"Everybody at Lienhofer's always texts about schedules and little problems that come up and stuff. Doesn't hurt to be friendly with coworkers. That's all it was."

Active held Apok's gaze a moment, his face showing nothing except a mild curiosity. "You ever give her a try, maybe get shut down?"

"No way, man," Apok said. "Those Kavoonah brothers, I don't need no drama with them. Anyway, you could tell Evie had big ideas. Girl like that I wouldn't mess with, nothing but trouble." Apok gazed into his Coke for a moment. "Maybe she found some trouble, all right. But I didn't have nothing to do with it. You don't think I did, do you, Danny?"

Kavik glanced at Active.

"We're just tying up some loose ends," Active said.

"It wasn't no accident like that report said, was it?" Apok's eyes moved between Active and Kavik.

"Just tying up some loose ends," Active said again. Then he studied his notebook for a few seconds. "What else? Oh, yeah—you happen to see anything out of the ordinary that night around the hangar, any kind of unusual activity, anybody hanging around you wouldn't normally see that time of night?"

"Nah, nothing. Nobody."

"Not even Cowboy?" Active scratched out a couple of lines in his notebook.

"Yeah, Cowboy, I must have seen him. And, maybe—maybe Pete."

"Pete Boskofsky? The pilot?"

Apok raised his eyebrows, yes. "Pete brings in a regular flight around nine or ten on Wednesdays."

"You remember it was Wednesday?" Active asked. "Something make it stand out in your mind?"

"Yeah," Apok said, "it was my kid's birthday. July sixth."

Apok pushed his chair back. "I answered your questions. I cooperated. Now, can you take me back home? I gotta get to work."

Active let out a slow breath. "Yeah, sure. Danny, maybe you could give Mr. Apok a ride."

The ramper jumped up and made the door in a couple of seconds.

"Say, Jesse." Active rose from his seat. "Just one more thing."

The ramper let go of the doorknob and his breath quickened.

"That girl who works at the weather station—she ever come around Lienhofer's?"

Apok's shoulders relaxed, and Active thought he saw the hint of a smile. "Yeah," he answered. "Monique. She's easy to remember."

"Nice-looking, ah?"

"Yeah." The ramper smirked. "Kinda crazy, though."

"How's that?"

"She got into it with Evie that one time. Like a couple of wild-cats." He put up a hand to mask a grin.

"Monique and Evie? I thought they didn't know each other."

"They know each other that time, all right. Monique grab Evie by the hair, say something to her. Then Evie, she smack that weather girl right in the face," Apok grinned again and rubbed his cheek. "Knocked her on her butt."

"What were they fighting about?"

"All I hear is Monique say, 'You're not going to have him.' Must be about some guy, ah?"

"What were you doing while all this was going on?" Active asked.

"Just watching, man, by the back door. They didn't know I was there."

"Back door of where?"

Apok's face froze for a second. "The hangar. At Lienhofer's."

"Monique was inside the hangar with Evie?"

Apok raised his eyebrows.

"And this was when?"

"Maybe late June. I remember we were hunting swans around then on them tundra ponds, back of the lagoon."

"What happened after Monique got decked?"

"Don't know. That little white dog was there. He saw me. He barked and I ducked out. I didn't need to be in the middle of no drama like that."

"Did you see Monique any other time?"

"Sure. She runs around the airfield sometimes when she's working at night."

"Sometimes when you're fueling up the planes?"

"Yeah, sometimes. She waves. I wave back."

"Do you remember seeing her the night before the plane crash?"

The ramper pursed his lips and frowned. "No, I never see her that night." He thrust his hands in his pockets and rolled his eyes. "I was kind of busy."

"Do you know what she does down at the weather station?"

He shrugged. "All I know is, she launches them white balloons. Pretty cool, ah?"

"Yeah, pretty cool," Active said. "All right, Jesse. Thanks for coming in."

Apok was already through the door.

"Hey, thanks for the dinner invite," Kavik said as Active pulled the Tahoe up to the house on the lagoon. "Caribou roast sounds pretty good."

"No problem. I figured you could use a break from taking care of your mom and your brothers and sisters."

"Yeah, there's not much more we can do for Mom at this stage except keep her comfortable. I guess they can get by without me for a couple of hours."

Active clapped Kavik on the shoulder. "Even caretakers need to be taken care of once in a while. That's what Grace keeps telling me, anyway." He stepped down from the Tahoe and swung up the rear window as Kavik climbed out of the passenger seat.

"Need some help?"

"No thanks." Active hoisted a thirty-pound bag of Puppy Chow to his shoulder and lowered the window shut.

"What's your take on our witnesses so far?" Kavik asked as they walked to the house. "You think they're hiding something?"

"Absolutely. Monique acted like she barely knew who Evie was, and she denied ever being in the Lienhofer hangar. But from what Jesse told us, they knew each other well enough to come to blows, and it happened in that hangar. Meanwhile, Jesse's lying about how much fuel he put in those tanks. Who do you think makes a better suspect?"

"I'd say Jesse. They both knew where to get the balloons, but he was the one who had the opportunity and the know-how to put them in the tanks."

Active nodded. "You know him better than me. Is he smart enough to come up with a plan like that?"

The front door flew open as they stepped onto the deck. A ball of yapping fur hurtled into Kavik's thigh.

"And here's Nita's new little friend," Active said. "I guess we can consider him a non-suspect."

"Could Jesse come up with a plan to bring down a plane?"

Kavik squatted and scratched the terrier's rump. "No way, not this elaborate, not without help"

"Like Monique, maybe."

"Like Monique."

The puppy bounced off Kavik's chin like it had springs on its paws, then jumped back up and slathered his face with its tongue.

Kavik grimaced and shut his eyes against the onslaught. "Hey, fella. I like you, too."

Laughing, he gripped the puppy by the whiskers on either side of his face and pushed him back.

"That brown eye makes him look like he's winking." He turned the dog's face toward Active.

Active studied it for a moment, then slapped his thighs. "Hey, Hercules!"

The dog launched off the floor, landed in Active's arms, and went to work on his face.

"Hercules, huh?" Kavik said.

"Not anymore. Now it's Lucky. Nita got him from Cowboy, who inherited him from Evie, who somehow got him after Monique gave him away."

Kavik gave him a puzzled frown. "Monique again? She's everywhere we look. Maybe she was the brains and Jesse was the brawn."

Active raised his eyebrows. "I've got a couple of assignments for you tomorrow."

"I thought I was checking around the airport for video surveillance tapes from that night."

"Alan Long can do that. I want you to run a background check on Ms. Monique Rogers. Then we're going to pay our weather balloon girl another visit."

CHAPTER NINE

• *Monday, August 22* •

HOME OF NATHAN AND GRACE ACTIVE, CHUKCHI

The front door opened and, then clicked shut after a few seconds. Lucky uncorked a high-pitched howl, followed by a burst of frenzied yips.

"Shhhhhh, shhhhhh," Nita hissed as she tried to corral the leaping terrier. She froze as the living room lights flicked on. The clock on the wall said five minutes before midnight.

Nathan and Grace faced her, shoulder to shoulder, arms folded.

Lucky paced in tight circles and panted.

"Guess you forgot about our new burglar alarm," Grace said. "Sit, little girl."

"I'm not a lit—" Nita protested.

"A good time to keep quiet, Nita," Active said.

She plopped onto the couch, clutched her phone to her chest, and pressed her knees together.

Grace stood over her, hands on hips, feet planted. "It's almost midnight. Where were you?"

"At Stacy's." Nita looked sideways.

"Really. Doing what?"

Nita huffed and drew her arms tighter across her chest. "Nothing. Listening to music, playing games and stuff."

"And stuff? Did we not discuss while we were having dinner with Officer Kavik that it was too late for you to go back out?"

"You discussed. I didn't. What's the big deal?"

Active sat down next to Nita. Lucky curled against her foot, eyes darting from one agitated human to the next.

"Listen, kiddo, you've got school tomorrow," Active said. "And more importantly, we don't want you wandering around at night by yourself, especially when we don't know where you are. I'm a cop, remember? Bad things can happen. I've seen 'em."

"Nothing happened, and I'm not a kid."

"You're thirteen," Grace fired back. "And that makes you a kid. And for the next two weeks, you are not leaving this house except for school."

The girl's mouth dropped open. "I'm grounded? The dance is next week, Mom. *Arii*, that's totally unfair!"

"And you can hand over that phone right now." Grace put out her hand. "No more texting with Stacy all night. Like I wasn't supposed to know about that either."

"You can't take my phone. That's a violation of my free speech!" Nita turned to Active with tearful eyes. "Tell her she can't do that."

Active air-pushed in the universal code for "take it down a notch."

"Actually, the phone is in my name, and we're your parents," Grace said. "So we *can* do that, and we *are* doing it." She bent forward and snatched the phone.

Nita collapsed into full-on wailing.

"You're not my parents!" she sobbed. "Why can't I have a real mom and dad?" She buried her face in her hands and her shoulders started to heave.

Grace sat down beside her on the opposite side from Active, put her arms around the crying girl and stroked her hair. "Honey, you *do* have a real mom and dad."

Nita raised her tear-streaked face but avoided eye contact. "I'm not blood, not like the baby." She paused a moment, catching her breath. "Stacy says being adopted isn't any better than being a foster kid like him. It's like I'm an orphan dog you took in, same as Lucky." She jumped up and darted into her bedroom. The dog shot through the door just before it slammed shut.

Grace and Active stared at each other across the empty space where Nita had been.

When Grace spoke, her voice shook. "How can I tell her that I *am* her real mother? I mean, the next question . . ."

"As in, 'Who is my father?'"

"Exactly. And I can't tell her that."

Her shoulders slumped and she spoke through gulping sobs. "Or why my sister killed herself and I ended up on the street—doing what I did—and . . ." She buried her face in her hands.

"Or that your mom—" Nathan said, stopping himself too late.

"That she what?" Grace's head was up now, eyes blazing through tears. "You mean that she took the blame for killing the bastard while she was dying of cancer to keep me out of jail?"

And there it was, the answer to the unspoken and unanswerable question that had always hovered over them like a ghost: Who did he really think had killed Jason Palmer?

He pushed into the sofa and thought back to the day Grace

had come home from Anchorage's notorious Four Street, the day her father was found shot to death in his office at Chukchi High, with all the evidence pointing to her. She was arrested and charged, but there had never been a trial. It had all been washed away when Ida Palmer, dying of cancer, was pushed into the courtroom in a wheelchair to confess to killing Jason Palmer, so he wouldn't do to Nita what he had done to his own daughters.

Active had loved Grace, even then, before he'd fully realized it. Had it kept him from facing the truth about a murder? Was it still?

The Chukchi city police chief at the time had put it in a nutshell during a post-mortem with Active when the case was over: "What kind of mother, if she's dying anyway, isn't gonna lie to keep her daughter from going to prison for killing the guy who raped her?"

"Well?" Grace said.

Who did he really think had killed Jason Palmer?

"I don't know," he said finally. "Some questions you just have to live with, I guess." He kissed her and she buried her face in his shoulder.

"I don't want Nita to have to carry all that history around with her," Grace said. "Like I do." She sat up. "Or the new baby. Am I putting another child through all of this? I don't think I could stand to—"

She collapsed back into his shoulder with a long sigh. Active stroked her arm.

"I don't have the answers, baby. But I know you'll figure it out. We will."

"I guess I should start seeing Nelda again."

"Always seemed like it helped before."

"You know, she supposedly comes from a long line of woman *angatquqs.*"

"Wherever she comes from, she's a very wise lady."

"If I talk to her about Nita and me, I don't know, maybe it'll all come clear, what to do." She patted her belly and studied it for a moment. "And about the baby and us, too." She was silent, then squeezed his hand. "I wasn't ready to have this child."

Active swallowed hard. "I know. And now?"

"I don't know. I mean, I'm not *not* ready."

Active frowned and abandoned the effort to navigate the labyrinths of the female psyche. Especially the pregnant female psyche. Hadn't this been decided before he'd made the big announcement to Martha?

"But Nita," Grace went on. "She's definitely not ready for this. She's still finding her place between you and me. A baby right now would—"

Nita's phone buzzed in Grace's hand. They looked at the screen to see a grinning teenager with a short Mohawk, deep dimples and a crooked front tooth.

"He is cute," Grace said.

The buzzing stopped and a text dinged in.

ruok? miss u. miss me? the message read.

Nita raced in with Lucky at her heels. Grace powered down the phone. Nita stared at it, then at Grace, then at Active, but said nothing. She looked ready to start bawling and bolt for her room again at any moment.

"Hey, kiddo." Active patted the space between himself and Grace. "Come, sit with us. Let's talk."

Nita hesitated, then sat down and drew in her arms and legs so that she didn't touch either grown-up. "About what?"

"About you and us and the baby," Grace said. "You don't feel like you belong in this family?"

"Your family is who you grow up with," Nita said. "I was already eleven when you adopted me."

"Oh, *bunnik*," said Grace. "There are two kinds of families, the one you're born into and the one you choose. We'll all be the family the baby is born into. But you, Nathan, me—we're the family who chose each other."

"But it's different."

"How?"

"If you were my real mom, I would be a part of you, because I came out of you. Blood is thicker than water. That's what Stacy says."

Grace looked at Active with fear in her eyes, swallowed hard, and took a deep breath. She looked at Nita. "Suppose I was your mother from birth."

Nita frowned. "But you're not."

Grace closed her eyes and took a deep breath.

"You're part of my heart. There's no way I could love you more. Blood, water, it doesn't matter. Only love matters."

Nita paused. "Will I be the baby's stepsister or adopted sister?"

"You'll be the baby's big sister. And you'll be great." Grace threw her arms around Nita. The girl stiffened but didn't pull away. "You know what? I have an ultrasound this week. Would you like to come with me?"

Nita shrugged and looked at the floor. "What for?"

"To get a look at your little sister or brother's heartbeat."

Nita shot a sideways glance at Grace with a skeptical frown. "You can see a heartbeat?"

"You can. It'll be a little pulse on the screen as the doctor moves the ultrasound wand across my tummy. So, you wanna come?"

Nita stretched a palm out to Lucky where he lay at her feet, head cocked as though taking in every word. The terrier licked the tips of her fingers. The girl shrugged again. "I guess so. But I'm kind of, like, grounded." She looked up at Grace and rolled her eyes.

Grace's face relaxed a little. Active couldn't tell if it was maternal tenderness or amusement at Nita's theatrics. Both, most likely.

"I'll make an exception in this case," she said.

Nita returned the smile and it turned into a huge yawn. "I'm tired. I'm going to bed." She stood up and brushed a strand of hair off her face. "Can I have my phone back?"

"Not until morning," Grace said.

"Am I still grounded for two whole weeks?"

Grace exchanged a look with Active. "Yes."

"But the dance," Nita whined.

"Two weeks," Grace repeated.

"But, M-o-o-om!"

"Two weeks," Grace and Active said in unison.

Nita stamped off to her room. Lucky trotted behind.

"Good night, sweetie," Grace called out.

Grace slid up against Active and laid her head on his shoulder.

He slumped back against the couch. "Hey, it's pretty late, and we both have work tomorrow. How about we get back to bed?"

"I'm too wound up for sleep. Maybe some herbal tea?"

"Sure."

A few minutes later, they sat at the kitchen table, Active staring into his cup and trying to keep his eyes open, Grace sipping with a faraway look.

"What's on your mind?" he asked.

"At least it'll be thirteen years before we have another teenager in the house."

Active laughed. "Amen to that."

CHAPTER TEN

• *Tuesday, August 23* •

WEATHER STATION, CHUKCHI

Monique, in her purple anorak, stood tapping frantically at a keyboard, when Active and Kavik walked into the weather station. As the door closed and cut off the whine of a biting late-summer wind, she cursed under her breath.

"Good morning, Ms. Rogers," Active said.

"Not from where I sit." She said it without turning. "This damn computer has been freezing up ever since I came in." She banged on the keyboard. "Damn! Damn! Damn!"

She whirled and stared at Active with an annoyed frown, then turned it on Kavik. "Who's this?"

"Danny Kavik, one of my officers, and we—"

"Look, Chief, I really don't have time for visitors right now."

"On your way out?"

She cocked her head and gave him a puzzled look.

"Your coat," he said.

"No, no." She shed the anorak and tossed it over the wooden bear. "I was a little cold earlier. But, seriously, I don't have time to chat."

"This is not a social call, Ms. Rogers. We need to ask you some questions."

"Like I told you, Chief, I got a little crisis going on here. Can we do this later?"

She dropped into her chair and threw a disgusted glance at the blank screen. Water pooled under a sweating, unopened Diet Pepsi beside the keyboard.

Active pulled a second chair toward the desk. "Afraid not, Ms. Rogers. We'd like to do this here, but we can ride up to Public Safety to do it there if you prefer. Strictly your choice."

Monique turned to face them and leaned on her thighs. "You *are* investigating that plane crash, aren't you?" She grabbed the soda and popped the top.

"Just filling in a few blanks." Active pulled a notebook from his jacket. "Isn't that your second Diet Pepsi this week?"

"Had a long night. I'm making an exception."

Kavik looked around the room and shifted on his feet. "That's some good-smelling coffee over there. Mind if I get some?"

"Help yourself." She waved at the pot. "Sorry I'm not in hospitality mode." She fished a yellow plastic straw out of a desk drawer, stuck it into the soda can, and took a long pull. "So what do you want from me?"

"We were wondering if you might want to correct anything you said yesterday."

Her eyes narrowed a little. "Like what?"

"Like anything that wasn't completely accurate."

Monique shrugged and did a good imitation of a bad actor doing confusion.

"I'm referring to your lack of recall about your interaction with Evie Kavoonah," Active said. "Seems like getting knocked off your feet might stick in your mind?"

Monique's mouth worked like a beached fish, but no sound came out.

"Who was the man you were fighting over?"

"M-man? There wasn't any man."

"You said, 'You're not going to have him,' right before she decked you. Who's 'him'?"

"Th-the dog. I told you I gave away my dog. I put an ad on Kay-Chuck, and she called. That's how we met."

"You get physical with a woman you just met. A couple of weeks later, she and her boyfriend end up dead. And you want me to believe your argument was about a dog?" Active said. "Maybe you can come up with a better story while we question you down at Public Safety. Shouldn't take more than two, three hours, right, Danny?"

Monique put out her hands as if to ward off a blow. Her eyes widened like a trapped animal's. "No, wait. I'll tell you what happened. Evie was the one who answered my ad and she came to get the dog."

"The truth, Ms. Rogers."

"That is the truth. I swear I never saw her before."

"And how did that turn into a fight?"

"Everything was cool at first. She was going to take Hercules. She asked if I had a problem with her changing his name. She thought maybe he should have a name he could live up to. I was okay with that. Then . . ." Tears welled up in her eyes. "She said she couldn't wait to show him to her boyfriend, Todd." Monique set her jaw, and the watery eyes turned to a smoldering gray.

"'Todd Brenner?' I asked her. 'Dr. Brenner?' She said, 'Yes, do you know him?'"

"Obviously you did."

"Obviously is right. Todd and I went out for about a month when he first moved to Chukchi." Monique glanced up toward the ceiling. She pressed her lips together, then relaxed her mouth as if she couldn't decide whether to cry or laugh. "It got serious pretty quick. I thought for a while maybe he was the one."

She shook her head and looked at Active again. "The one! Can you believe it? What a fool I—" She paused. "Then all of a sudden, he wants to put things on ice. He said he just broke up with some woman he was supposed to marry in Texas and he wasn't ready for a serious relationship yet. He wanted some space, maybe sometime in the future, he said. I was willing to wait . . ." She put a hand over her trembling mouth.

"And then it turned out he was ready to be serious about Evie, just not about you?"

"That's why I couldn't talk about it when you asked me about Evie." Her tears welled up again. "I come all the way up here to get over a broken heart, and then . . ." She dabbed at the corner of one eye. "And then history repeats itself. It's so . . . humiliating."

She sniffled, then cocked an eyebrow. "Who told you about the fight?"

"We had a talk with your friend."

She stared back in silence, the eyebrow still arched like a question mark.

"Jesse Apok."

"Jesse? That weasel!" Her dark eyes blazed.

Active waited for her to boil over with more information, but she went silent and sank back into her chair.

Kavik walked back to refill his mug, then leaned on the counter by the coffee pot.

"He talked like the two of you were pretty friendly," Active said.

"Seriously? Jesse?" Her cheeks caved in as she sucked at the soda. "Not exactly my type."

"Stranger things have happened," Kavik said, smiling into his coffee.

"Uh-huh," Active said. "We got the impression the two of you hung out some."

"Jesse said that? He's a liar."

Active scratched in his notebook, then turned his gaze back on Monique. "That's not the only thing about your, ah, reliability, Ms. Rogers. You said you'd never been in the Lienhofer hangar?"

"I haven't!" She leaned forward, as if about to lunge.

"Not according to Jesse. He said that's where he saw you get in Evie's face and get knocked on your butt."

"Oh, he did, did he?" Monique tossed back the mass of dark curls as if to shake away the questions. "I invited Evie down here to pick up Hercules. She asked what I did, and, when I told her, she wanted me to show her how I launch the balloons. We met in the garage."

"Not in the hangar? Why would Jesse lie about that?" Active scrawled in his notebook again.

Monique squinted. "Because the little snake didn't want anyone asking why he came down here."

"And why did he?" Active asked. "He want a tour of your operation, too? See where you keep the balloons and how you do a launch?"

"Yeah, sure, I showed him around one time. And he was real interested. But that's not what I'm talking about." Monique pushed her tongue against her cheek. "He kept a bottle of Smirnoff in a hole he'd dug against the back wall of my garage. He would come down here on his four-wheeler for a swig when things got slow at Lienhofer's. Then I caught him and told him to knock it off or I would report him to his boss. Apparently, ratting me out about the thing with Evie is his idea of payback. The little shit."

"All right, let's get back to that, then." Active said. "The Evie situation. You've got a good thing going with a handsome young doctor, then a little village girl steals him away. When you confront her about it, she lands the first punch and it's even more humiliating. You couldn't let it go, right? You said she couldn't have him."

"Yeah, I was a little hot about it at first, finding out like that. Everyone says things in the heat of the moment. I'm sure, even you . . . anyway, I didn't have her arrested for assault, and I let her have the dog. Doesn't that prove I don't carry a grudge?"

"Not necessarily. Maybe you needed time to think about how to get even. Maybe you thought if you couldn't have Todd, neither could Evie."

Monique took another long slug of soda that sucked the can dry. "No way. There are other fish in the sea—with bigger fins."

She raised her eyebrows and grinned at her own joke. Active and Kavik didn't.

"I understand you didn't give up that easy in Fresno last year?" Active said.

Her eyes widened. "How did you find out—"

Active smiled. "We're cops, is how."

"Something about stalking, a restraining order?" Kavik prodded.

Monique shot him a look like she'd just remembered he was in the room.

"Somebody at your gym?" Kavik went on. "Fairly major situation, sounds like?"

Monique froze for a couple of seconds, then waved her hand in dismissal. "That was just a misunderstanding."

"It always is," Kavik said. "Some property damage, too, wasn't there? What was that all about?"

"That charge was dismissed," Monique said with a shrug. "And it wasn't like his car was new."

"You keyed someone's car?" Kavik asked.

Monique smiled. "Please. What I did was—" She paused and smiled. "I filled a couple of balloons with paint and splattered his Beamer. It's not like I hurt him."

Active and Kavik traded looks.

"And you didn't want to do anything to Todd and Evie?" Active asked.

"Like punch them?"

Active stared at her for a beat. "I'm not talking about assault, Ms. Rogers. Todd dumped you for another woman, and now they're both dead. You see what I'm saying?"

Monique stared blankly, then slammed the empty soda can on the desk and jumped to her feet. "You think I brought down that plane because Todd ditched me for Evie Kavoonah? That's crazy! I never would have wished anything like that on anyone. And even if I did, I wouldn't know how to do it. The only thing I know how to fly is a weather balloon."

Active and Kavik exchanged glances.

Kavik moved toward the window behind Monique's desk and took a closer look at the photo of the terrier.

"What a cutie." Kavik paused but got no response. "They say a dog can really ease the stress in a person's life."

"I run," Monique said.

"Jesse said he's seen you running alongside the airfield at night sometimes."

"So? I already told Chief Active that."

Kavik walked back to the desk. "You see Jesse while you were out running the night before the crash?"

"Your boss already asked me that." The computer screen behind her came to life and began scrolling bar graphs and columns of numbers. She glanced behind her, then pointed at a red light blinking on her phone. "I think that's a message from my IT guy in Fairbanks. Are we done here?"

"Sometimes, when I'm trying to remember something, I picture what I was doing at the time, like playing a movie in my head," Kavik offered.

Monique pressed her fingers to her temples.

"Jesse would have been around a purple and white Cessna, high wing, single prop, outside the Lienhofer hangar," Kavik added. "Maybe fueling it up. Remember anything like that?"

"You think he did something to that plane?"

"So you did see him?" Active asked, pen poised over the notebook.

"Yeah. He was on a ladder up at the wing. I guess he could have been fueling the plane, but, like I told you, I don't know anything about planes."

"Right, just balloons," Active said.

Monique nodded. "Just balloons."

Active and Kavik paused outside the weather-station door and gazed across the airport in thought.

"Well," Kavik said, "one of them is lying."

"If not both. Question is—" Active's phone bleated from his jacket pocket. He pulled it out and checked the caller ID.

"Yeah, Alan."

He listened for a moment, said "On the way," and tapped off.

Kavik looked at him, eyebrows raised in the white expression of inquiry.

"Jesse Apok's dead."

CHAPTER ELEVEN

• *Tuesday, August 23* •

PAMIUKTUK STREET APARTMENTS, CHUKCHI

The first thing Active noticed about Jesse Apok's apartment was the gunmetal smell of blood. It was so familiar now, so instantly recognizable, that it made him wonder again if it was time to find a new line of work.

He shook his head, covered his nose and mouth with his handkerchief, and stepped through the door.

The source of the smell lay on the kitchen floor, still in an overturned chair, empty eyes fixed on the blood-spattered ceiling. A pool of brown-red blood mixed with brain matter and bone fragments had congealed under his head on the stained, holed linoleum.

His arms loosely embraced the barrel of a hunting rifle propped between his bent legs. The muzzle pointed toward a hole under his chin where the bullet had begun its swift, deadly journey. Pale bare feet protruded from the frayed cuffs of his jeans.

Kavik moved around the room, taking photos, then moved in and circled the corpse for close-ups.

Active pocketed the handkerchief—his brain had processed the smell and no longer noticed it now—and leaned over the kitchen table. He searched for blood at the edge of the table closest to the fallen body but found none. He stood up and surveyed two empty Smirnoff bottles that lay on the table beside a sardine can filled with ashes and cigarettes smoked down to the filter.

"How do you think it played out?"

"First impression?" Kavik said. "He's sitting at the table, drinking himself stupid. He's got the gun between his knees. He puts the muzzle under his chin, pulls the trigger, and falls backward in the chair. Basic village suicide."

Active circled the table. He eyeballed the distance between the upturned feet of the corpse and the edge of the table. "This chair was maybe two feet from the table. Who sits that far back when they're trying to drink away their troubles?"

Kavik rubbed his jaw. "Okay, so maybe he pushed back to get the gun between his legs. What difference does it make?"

"Like the wise man said, everything should be made as simple as possible. But not more so."

"Yeah, okay," Kavik said. "Message received."

Active pulled on latex gloves. As Kavik photographed the items on the table and the floor beneath, Active squatted near the body, studying its position and taking notes.

Then he worked the bolt on the rifle and extracted a single spent cartridge, which he put in a Ziploc bag from his pocket. The rifle went into a big plastic trash bag from Kavik's pack, and the Smirnoff bottles into another trash bag.

"Give this stuff to Long," he told Kavik. "I'm going to take a look around the place. You should talk to the neighbor who called it in."

A heavyset, fifty-ish Inupiat woman with big glasses and an orange-and-pink-flowered *atiqluk* stood with Alan Long just outside the open door of Apok's first-floor unit in the eight-plex. She pressed her palms to her cheeks and shook her head as Kavik approached. "*Arii,* that Jesse," Active heard her say. "I always tell him he'll end up like this. All the time too much drinking, that guy."

Active surveyed the tiny kitchen. An unwashed coffee pot on the counter; a plate, knife, and fork, also unwashed, in the sink.

Clipped onto the refrigerator door with a magnet was a photo of a smiling Apok with a grinning toddler on his shoulders. Another picture, slightly blurry, showed him in a boat with the little boy between his legs. A man about Apok's age, but heavier and vaguely familiar, stood behind him, mugging and stretching out his arms like a goofy bird.

The rest of the refrigerator door was decorated with spidery crayon drawings. Stick animals that looked a little like caribou, a small boy holding a man's hand, the same boy holding a woman's hand—but none of the boy standing between the man and woman, holding hands with both.

In the bedroom, Active found a double bed sans headboard and sheets, a green nylon-covered sleeping bag on top, and mismatched pillows without cases. A lamp with a tilted shade stood on the nightstand. In one corner, a big plastic tote held a toy dump truck, plastic blocks, a Spider-Man action figure, and a mixing bowl full of Legos.

In the bathroom, a dirty toilet with the seat up stood next to a slightly cleaner tub with a flimsy white plastic shower curtain. A yellow rubber duck perched in a corner of the tub next to a bottle of dandruff shampoo. On the rim of the sink, a Scooby-Doo tooth-brush leaned against a larger one in a blue cup.

As Active left the bedroom, Kavik came in with the two para-medics who had been first on the scene, then stepped out when the officers arrived to investigate.

"Ready, Chief?" one asked as they brought in a gurney.

"All yours," Active said.

"Crime lab, right?" The paramedic dropped the gurney's wheels.

"Absolutely."

Active joined Kavik in the kitchen as the paramedics loaded Apok's body onto the gurney, covered him with a sheet, and rolled him out the front door.

"Long talked to the upstairs neighbor, Dolly Swanson," Kavik said. "I went over it again with her just now. She heard loud voices coming from downstairs early this morning. Maybe men's voices, or they could have been male and female."

"Someone else was here?"

"Or it could have been the TV. Apparently Apok kept it blasting whenever he was here and they had words about it a couple times. She didn't see anyone go in or out and no other cars other than the usual. Things quieted down after a while and she stretched out on the couch for a nap about nine—she says she was up late babysit-ting the grandkids. She thinks she had just dozed off when she heard a loud bang from Jesse's unit. She thought it was a dream or maybe his TV again, so she let it go. But she kept thinking about it and finally around noon decided maybe it was a gunshot. She knocked on his door, then called 911 when he didn't answer."

"So Jesse was dead for maybe three hours when the body was found," Active said. "We have a pretty good idea of how he died and when. But nothing that tells us why. Or who."

"Who? Not a suicide, then?"

Active ran a hand through his hair. "That's what it looks like, but—"

"But someone could have helped Jesse with the gun."

"Exactly. It fits with our theory of Monique as the brains and Jesse as the brawn."

Kavik nodded. "Monique uses Jesse to bring down the plane. Maybe he tells her we questioned him, and she decides he's gonna fold and she has to take care of it. But we just talked to her. You're thinking she could have been here earlier this morning?"

"It's possible. She said she was having computer problems all morning, but she was still wearing her anorak when we came in."

"Right. She said she was cold."

"And yet she's got a cold soda sitting on her desk ready to drink?"

"Yeah, that is weird," Kavik said. "Maybe she is our killer."

"In which case we now have three homicides," Active said. "Evie, Todd, and Jesse, all killed by Monique. Or, maybe Jesse Apok killed Jesse Apok. Let's take another look."

They stepped back in and Active surveyed the living room. A big widescreen TV, the only thing that looked new, balanced on a plastic stand against a curtainless window. Across from the TV, a worn brown sofa slumped against a wall under a wood-and-ivory crucifix and a seven-foot frond of blue-gray baleen feathered along the lower edge. On a spindly table next to the couch sat a well-thumbed Bible, open to a page marked with a faded red ribbon.

"Not much here," Kavik said.

"Not of a life. You a religious man?"

Kavik shrugged. "I take Mom to church sometimes, say 'amen' at the right time."

Active pointed at the Bible. "See if anything jumps out that could put us inside Mr. Apok's head. I'm going to take another swing through the kitchen."

Active stepped around the bloodstains on the floor and opened the back door. To his right, a wheel-less bicycle frame and a small, banged-up motorcycle leaned against the wall, almost hidden in tall weeds.

An older apartment building stood back to back with the Pamiuktuk. A couple of pickups were parked in the space between, one collapsed onto its tires. Three teenagers traded shots at a bare basketball hoop. Active walked over, asked a few questions, and learned they had only arrived a half hour earlier and hadn't seen anything out of the ordinary.

He returned to the apartment and stared again at the refrigerator with its photo of Jesse Apok and his son. They had the same grin.

He moved up for a closer look and noticed a smudge on the boy's face. A stroke from a thumb? Or maybe a print from a kiss? As he removed the photo and slid it into a baggie, the toe of his shoe nudged something on the floor just under the refrigerator door. He knelt and pulled out a silver flip phone.

Kavik came into the kitchen with the Bible in his hand, still open to the page marked with the ribbon. "I may have something here, Chief. James, chapter five, verse sixteen: 'Confess your faults one to another and pray one for another that ye may be healed.'"

"Maybe Jesse was in a confessional state of mind." Active opened the phone, checked the screen, and handed it to Kavik.

The screen showed a text marked UNDELIVERABLE and sent at 9:12 A.M. to "Evie."

Kavik read it out loud: "Sorry."

CHAPTER TWELVE

• *Tuesday, August 23* •

HOME OF DENISE SHELDON, CHUKCHI

"*Arii!* It's my fault!" Denise Sheldon clutched a pillow to her chest and toppled sideways onto the stained gray sofa. The toddler clutching her leg began to bawl.

"Sorry for your loss, Ms. Sheldon." Active perched on an unsteady wooden chair and balanced his notebook on a knee.

Minutes earlier, he and Danny Kavik had reached the plywood-sided house with its faded blue paint off the north end of Beach Street, not far from the crisis center Grace managed, and informed Jesse Apok's ex-girlfriend of his death. "Sometimes people always blame theirself when somebody die." Active realized he was subconsciously matching Denise's Village English and yanked himself back. "Danny and I could really use your help understanding what happened to Jesse. We can step outside if you need a little time."

Denise glanced up and muffled her cries with the pillow.

"Ms. Sheldon, can I get you some water?" Kavik offered.

Denise shook her head and rubbed puffy eyes with the backs of chubby hands.

An older but thinner woman with the same button nose and dimpled cheeks came in and lifted the toddler. As they rubbed noses, Active realized he was the boy in the photo on Apok's refrigerator.

"No more crying, *kuukuung*. You come with *aana* and let your *aaka* talk to these men."

Denise pushed herself upright and snuffled as her mother carried the child out. His wails subsided and cartoon characters began to sing from a TV in a back room.

"I'm ready." She brushed long, tangled black hair, streaked with crimson, away from her face.

Active passed her his handkerchief. She blew her nose loudly and balled the handkerchief in her fist. She straightened an oversized flowered blouse, folded her hands in her lap, and pressed her thick, jean-clad thighs together.

"When was the last time you talked to him?" Active asked.

"This morning, right before he—*arii*, I should have let him see Corey like he wanted, he, he—"

"That's a really cute boy you've got there," Kavik said. "He's, what, about three maybe?"

Denise nodded and dabbed her eyes with a dry corner of the handkerchief.

"Can you be more specific about the time?" Active continued after a couple of seconds.

"Lemme think," Denise said. "It was about seven this morning he call me. I'm just getting home from my shift at the Arctic Inn."

"What do you do there?"

"I'm the night clerk, I run the front desk and input the

financial information for the day. The night shift pays two dollars an hour extra."

"And Jesse called you about seven?"

"Yeah," Denise said. "He was crying and really drunk already, even that early. He said he did something bad and he couldn't live with it no more."

"Did he say what it was?"

"No, I ask him, 'Jesse, what did you do?' But he never tell me." She teared up and pinched the corners of her eyes. "He just beg me to let him see Corey, like he won't be seeing him for a long time. I say, 'Jesse, you're really scare me now.' He just keep asking to see Corey. So I say, 'Okay, Jesse, but you don't do nothing crazy.'"

Active scrawled in his notebook. "And you went to his apartment?"

Denise took two deep breaths, nodded, and wiped at her nose with the handkerchief. "I drove over with the baby."

"What time was this?"

"Probably we got there fifteen minutes later. Around seven-thirty maybe."

Active noted the time and put a question mark beside it. "What happened then?"

"I sit in my car for maybe twenty minutes and think about how that Jesse is always being bossy, always trying to get his way. I call him on my cell and he sounds too drunk, all right. I tell him, 'I'm not letting you see Corey when you're like this.'"

"What did he say?"

"He just cry and say it's not right he can't see his son and then he's cursing and saying more stuff about how he can't live with himself."

"Did he mean suicide?"

"No . . . I don't know. He always get drunk and say crazy things like 'my gun is my one true friend, my gun never fuck me over like a woman.' I ask him where his gun is and he say, 'same place as always.'"

"Where was that?"

"In his bedroom closet."

"And the shells?"

"Same place." She nodded.

Active paused for a few moments. "When you were talking to him on the phone, did you hear anyone else in the background?"

Denise flicked her eyes upward in thought. "Yeah, the TV, sound like."

"Male voice? Female voice?"

She tapped her knee. "Both, all right. But I know it was the TV. Jesse wouldn't have no woman in there. He never want any girl but me, not even after we break up. I know lotta girls think that, but with Jesse it was true." She twirled a strand of the crimson hair around a finger, then unwound it. "It had to be the TV. He always have that TV on."

"He ever mention a girl named Monique?"

"Monique? Uh-uh." Denise's eyes narrowed. "Why? Who's that?"

Active let the question go unanswered. "Did he ever say anything about anybody at the weather station?"

Denise bit her lower lip and gazed into an unseen distance for a moment. "One time he talk about them weather balloons, say he will take Corey sometime to watch them go up. Is Monique from the weather station?"

"Yeah, we think she and Jesse talked sometimes. She knew he

hid a bottle of vodka behind her building and he'd slip down there for a drink while he was at work. Maybe they shared a sip now and then, maybe he told her something that would help us understand why he did this."

Denise crossed her arms and glared. "Why don't you ask her, then?"

"Good idea, Ms. Sheldon." Active pretended to note it down. "So you asked Jesse about his gun. Did you keep talking after that?"

"No. The call dropped or he hung up. I try calling him back but it go right to voicemail. Corey start fussing, so I come home."

Small feet pattered into the room. The toddler scrambled onto the couch, buried his face in his mother's breast, then peeked out at Kavik with a tentative grin. Kavik smiled back.

Denise's lower lip trembled. "*Arii*, it's my fault. I should have done something. If I knock on his door to see if he's okay . . ." She buried her face in her hands and snuffled.

"Then you and this little guy might not be with us this afternoon," Kavik said.

Denise raised her tear-streaked face and shifted the child on her lap. "He wouldn't ever hurt me or the baby."

"You never know when someone's been drinking," Kavik said. "They can make bad decisions. Especially if there's a gun around."

"Did you ever feel like hurting him?" Active asked.

Denise dabbed at her eyes. "*Arii*, Jesse and I always fight, all right, but not like that. Sometimes he'll give me hard time about the child support, but now he's gone, I'll have to get a second job. You know, I take care of my mom, too. I never want him dead."

"When you couldn't get Jesse on the phone, did you call anyone else?" Active asked.

"No. Oh, my god, I should have called Paul. He would have helped."

"Paul?" Kavik asked.

"Paul Noyakuk. They're friends since grade school. They always hang out, go hunting, go fishing, except when Paul was in the military and then not so much when he's back, even after Jesse get him that job at Lienhofer's."

"Ah," Kavik said. "He's their janitor, right?"

Denise raised her eyebrows, yes.

Active wrote the name in his notebook. "You say they weren't hanging out like before. Did they have a falling out?"

"No, nothing like that. Paul, he always get real moody, don't want to be around nobody." Denise clapped her palms to her cheeks. "Oh, my God. I don't want him to find out about Jesse from someone at work. I have to call him."

"Call Unca Paw," the boy sang out.

"Yes, Corey, we're going to call Akkaga Paw," Denise kissed the top of the toddler's head.

The boy grinned again at Kavik. "Go fishing with Daddy and Unca Paw." His black eyes sparkled.

Denise stroked the dark, silky hair around her son's ear as she thumbed the screen of her phone. She listened, shook her head, and left a voicemail asking Noyakuk to call her.

Suddenly, Active remembered the photo on Jesse Apok's refrigerator. The blurry Inupiaq imitating a bird had to be Paul Noyakuk.

"I'll bet you're a good fisherman." Kavik winked at the boy. "Catch a lotta fish, ah?"

Corey nodded. "Lotta fish. With Daddy and Unca Paw."

Active put away his notebook. "I don't think we have any more questions right now, Ms. Sheldon." He handed her a business card.

"Will you call me if you think of anything else that might help us understand what Jesse did?"

Denise took the card and held out his handkerchief.

He air-pushed it back to her. "It's okay, you keep it. I've got lots."

She squinted the Inupiat no. "I could wash it and call you, ah?"

"So," Kavik said as they climbed into Active's SUV. "Suicide after all?"

"Probably." Active slid behind the steering wheel and started the engine. "Maybe."

"You heard her. Jesse wanted to kill himself because he did something bad. Meaning he must have sabotaged the plane, right?"

Active shrugged. "Or he thought he screwed up and didn't put in enough fuel that night. Or he was torn up over something we don't even know about yet. And was he telling Denise he wanted to kill himself, or just venting to get whatever it was off his chest?"

Kavik shook his head. "Time to talk to his buddy, ah?"

Active nodded and turned south down Beach Street toward the airport. "And while we're talking to Noyakuk, let's ask him if Jesse mentioned Monique."

"Yeah, funny how those balloons keep coming up every time we question somebody."

Active looked west over the Chukchi seawall. It had been put in a couple of years earlier to defend the village against the pack ice that rode in on the brutal fall storms that seemed to get worse every year. But there was no ice now, not in late August, just the blue-gray waves of the Chukchi Sea slapping against the stone face of the wall. A half mile out, two hunters headed up-country in an aluminum dory with a big white outboard on the back.

Kavik's voice brought Active back to the business at hand.

"That text on the phone, though. It sure seems like a suicide note, ah?"

"Yeah," Active said. "Assuming Jesse wrote it."

"Afternoon," Active called as he knocked on the half-open office door of the co-owner of Lienhofer Aviation.

Delilah Lienhofer looked up with a scowl that would stop a charging grizzly. "What's so fucking good about it?"

Active was reminded of why Cowboy called her the Dragon Lady and decided against pointing out that he had actually not called the afternoon 'good.' Kavik, he noticed as they stepped into the office, kept some distance back. Was he really using Active as a shield against Delilah?

"At least we're having a better afternoon than Jesse Apok," Active said.

Delilah's scowl deepened under a thick helmet of mouse-colored hair. "Jesse Apok. He's the reason my day is in the shitter."

She huffed out an exasperated breath. "No disrespect to the dead, but I have six flights still on the schedule today, and I've lost my ramper. I had to call Leon Fox in to work a double shift, so I'm on the hook for the overtime."

She shook her head, and something between bewilderment and compassion crossed her face. "Life's a bitch, I guess, but what makes a person give up on it like that?"

"That's what we're trying to figure out. We need to talk to one of your employees."

"Yeah? Who's that?"

"Paul Noyakuk," Active said. "He around?"

Delilah looked like she was about to spit across the room. "That little shit. He's another one didn't show up for work today. I had to find out from Pete Boskofsky. He talked to Pete last night, said he was going caribou hunting up the Katonak today."

"How long?"

"Couple days, maybe. Who knows with these guys?"

"He didn't put in for time off?"

"In Chukchi? When the caribou show up, off they go. No leave request, not even the courtesy of a decent lie about a sick *aana* or something. Apparently I'm running a fucking volunteer camp here. Should have hired the fucking Koreans to clean this place."

"Paul's your janitor, right?"

"Yeah. Too bad he didn't work out as a ramper, I could sure as hell use him right now."

"He was a ramper?"

"We tried him out for a month—you know, support the troops, hire a vet. But the mechanics and pilots couldn't work with him. Too sullen and kinda fucked up in the head, like a lot of these village kids when they come home from whatever sand dune we're bombing this week. So we gave him a job where he could make his own schedule, which he apparently takes to mean it's optional to show up at all."

She stopped and her face lost a little of its color. "Sorry," she said after a few seconds. "It all just kinda piles up on you sometimes."

"Understandable," he said. "Perfectly understandable. So, Jesse and Paul—they were pretty tight?"

Delilah shrugged. "Supposedly. Wouldn't know, other than Jesse vouched for him when he applied for the job."

"Okay," Active said, "we'll try again when Noyakuk's back in town. I hope your day gets better."

The scowl from hell was back. "Fat fucking chance."

As Active and Kavik walked toward the Tahoe, a voice yelled "Hang on!" and Cowboy Decker hurried over from across the parking lot.

"What the hell's going on?" the pilot growled. "Jesse Apok shot himself?"

"I see the tundra telegraph is working overtime today," Active said. "We're investigating."

"It's a suicide, obviously?"

"Maybe. We're investigating."

"You were going to question him, right? Did he have something to do with Evie and Todd being killed?"

"Like I said, we're investigating. And you know I can't talk to you about it."

Cowboy snorted. "There wouldn't be any damn investigation if it wasn't for me pushing on it."

"I know. But now there is one, and I can't talk about it."

Cowboy jabbed a finger into Active's chest. "Because I'm still a suspect?"

"Because it's an investigation."

"Jesse was the last one who had access to those tanks," Cowboy said. "You think he put in those balloons and knew you were onto him, and that's why he committed suicide?"

Active gave a noncommittal shrug.

Cowboy stared at the ground for a few seconds as the wind spun up a small dust devil. "Why would Jesse Apok want to kill

Todd or Evie, assuming he even knew she was gonna be in the plane?"

"Unless it was you he was after." Active said. "Last thing he knew, it was supposed to be you with Todd, right?"

Cowboy tossed the cigarette into the gravel and ground it out. "Makes no fucking sense," he snarled. "Nothing does now."

CHAPTER THIRTEEN

• Wednesday, August 24 •

NEAR THE ACTIVE HOME, CHUKCHI

Active handed Grace a paper cup of chai tea as she finished zipping up her jacket and they started their walk along the lagoon. A few ducks bobbed at the edge of the water. Gold-leafed aspens shivered in a sudden gust and sprayed leaves across a carpet of wet tundra that showed the first hint of autumn rust.

He took a sip of coffee, let the steam from the opening in the plastic lid swirl up against his face. "So how often are we doing this?"

"Three times a week, at least. I'm exercising for two. The baby's heartbeat was so strong on the ultrasound! I want to make sure we both stay in good shape."

"And I'm here because . . . ?"

"Because you're keeping your honey company. And a walk will do you some good, too." She reached over and patted his middle. "I'm not the only one getting a little paunchy."

"Is that so?" he said with a grin. Her quicksilver eyes sparkled up at him. A rosy glow made her tawny skin even more luminous than usual. He flicked back a strand of hair that had blown across her face and caught at the corner of her mouth. "You're beautiful when you're pregnant, Grace Palmer Active."

She drained her cup, stuffed it in a pocket, and kissed him. "That's very kind." She whirled around. "Now, let's move it." She took off in a power walk, arms pumping.

Active quick-stepped to catch up. "Hey, did you and Nelda have a good talk?"

"Not exactly. She was on her way to Cape Goodwin for a funeral. We had maybe ten minutes."

"And nine and a half of that was exchanging greetings."

"And interstitial silences. You don't rush an elder." Grace slowed her pace. "But she said something interesting."

"Like?"

"When there's mourning for a death, there's more reason to celebrate a life."

"Wow. Where'd that come from?"

Grace looked down and shrugged. "I told her I was two-minded when I found out I was pregnant.'"

"But now you're not, right?" He suppressed his frustration—and his alarm—at having to ask this again.

She nodded thoughtfully. "I keep thinking about that night in the tent on the Hawk River."

"Yeah," he said with a slow, satisfied smile. "That was excel—"

She dropped his hand and slapped his shoulder. "Not that. My dream."

"Right. You were falling out of the sky."

"Yeah. And what I keep thinking about is, Evie really did fall out of the sky and lose her baby. I don't know how to explain it, but when I think about being there, below that ridge where she and her baby died, I feel like, no matter how afraid I am about not getting motherhood right this time either, it's like this baby deserves its chance because Evie's baby never got one. Does that make sense?"

"Yeah, kind of like what Nelda was saying, her death makes that little life you're carrying that much more important."

She smiled and hugged his arm. "It's not true, what women say."

"Eh?"

"A man *can* have a clue about what a pregnant woman goes through."

"We have our moments, I suppose." He pulled up his collar against the wind off the water. "So you're talking to Nelda again when she gets back?"

"Absolutely. And she wants you there, too. Shared therapy."

"Glad to know you're feeling more sure about the pregnancy," he said. "I was a little worried."

"I've been getting my checkups, eating right, taking walks, all the mommy stuff. I thought you'd get the message."

"Maybe I'm not as much in tune as you give me credit for."

"Or maybe investigating a double homicide requires a little focus? I can see where it might."

She smiled up at him and gave his arm another squeeze, and he understood the subject had changed.

"Yeah, two deaths, too many things that don't add up," he said.

"And now that suicide, Jesse Apok."

"Yeah," Active said, "And the thing is, Jesse's death could be connected to the plane crash. He was the guy who fueled up the plane. So he could have screwed up somehow, or even sabotaged it. But, of course, he's not talking now and, so far, there seem to be no witnesses to anything unusual that night."

"No one at the airport?"

"We were hoping surveillance video might show something, but most of the cameras weren't hooked up, and the ones that were don't cover Lienhofer's tarmac."

"Security, Chukchi-style."

"Absolutely. And Alan Long and Danny and I talked to the Lienhofer employees—nothing. Of course, most of 'em work the day shift, so they weren't around that night."

"Nothing even from Cowboy?"

"No," Active said. "Jesse said he saw Cowboy and one of the other pilots, Pete Boskofsky, there that night. But Cowboy says he left before Jesse came on shift and Long found out that Pete, who normally makes a run on Wednesdays, was in Kenai on family business."

"So maybe Jesse mixed his nights up? Maybe he wasn't there at all that night?"

"He seemed pretty sure about it. And we do have a sighting from the woman who works nights down at the weather station. But all she can confirm is that she saw him on a ladder at the wing, maybe fueling the plane, which is where he would have been if he was doing his job." He looked across the lagoon. The wind rippled the gray-blue water. "How far is it around this side of the lagoon?"

"And this woman is a reliable witness?"

Monique Rogers, reliable? "Up to a point."

"What point?"

He chuckled. "The point where she opens her mouth, basically."

She gave his jacket sleeve a little tug. "Luckily, you don't have to worry about that with me."

He smiled and squeezed her arm against his side.

"You said Jesse's death might be connected to the plane crash?"

"There could be a second person involved in that crash who thought he might talk about it."

"You're saying Jesse was murdered to keep him from talking?"

"It's possible. But we don't have any concrete evidence for it. No witnesses to anyone else being in his apartment at the time. I'm waiting for the crime lab in Anchorage to come back with identification of the fingerprints on the rifle he was killed with or the cell phone we found at the scene, maybe something on his body or on that balloon from the 207's fuel tank. Just hunches at this point."

"You're still going with the water balloon theory?"

"Yeah, Danny and I tested it out this morning on the one balloon I kept from the crash. It took twenty-three and a half gallons of water, no problem, which would leave room for seven or eight gallons of fuel per tank, just like Cowboy figured."

"So you think that balloon you sent to the lab will lead you to the murderer?"

"Maybe. If they don't lose it."

"Three quarters of a mile."

Active paused for a few seconds, hit his mental rewind button, and remembered the question she was answering.

"Ah," he said. "Around the side of the lagoon." It was crazy how she could calculate that on sight, which he suspected was the point.

"You wimping out?" she said with a grin.

"No chance."

He figured they had walked just under a quarter mile, meaning a half mile to go.

"But, you know, the case. I might get a phone call and have to get back to work."

"Work. Okay, that might get you off the hook. So let's kick it into gear before that happens."

Grace threw back her head and took off again, elbows chopping the air and heels flipping up. The white soles of her shoes looked like the undersides of the tails of leaping caribou.

"Hey, hold up, speedy." Active jogged up beside her and checked the temptation to break into a full run to show her which of them was out of shape.

As he came alongside, a cell phone bleated from one of their pockets.

"You didn't arrange with Public Safety to make a rescue call to get you out of this, did you? That had better not be Lucy Brophy. Seriously."

Active fished in his pocket for his cell and pulled it out. "Ha! Not me."

Grace retrieved the phone from her jacket, frowned at the caller ID, and put it to her ear. Her eyes widened, then she rubbed her forehead and said, "What? Why?" She listened for another few seconds, then said, "Okay, we're on our way."

She tapped off. Active raised his eyebrows in the *naluaqmiut* expression of inquiry.

"We have to go to the school. Nita got sent to the principal's office."

"For what?"

Grace's eyes burned with anger.

"She punched a girl."

• • •

Nita was slumped in a red plastic chair, eyes puffy from crying, hiccupping intermittently and wiping her nose on the sleeve of her hoodie. An angry red scratch ran across one cheek.

"Oh, Dad!" she cried as Active stepped into the principal's office. She launched out of the chair, threw herself into his arms, and sobbed. The frown on Grace's face got a little deeper. Was the girl parent-shopping in her moment of crisis?

Active folded her into his chest and cradled a hand around the back of her head. How small it was; sometimes he forgot she was still only a child. And the way she had said, "Dad." The word had come to feel less awkward since their talk on the Hawk River. But now, the weight of responsibility that came with it paralyzed him.

Maybe Grace would know what to do.

Their eyes met over Nita's head for a second. He thought Grace might reach out to the girl, turn her around, and embrace her.

Instead, she pulled one of the red chairs up to the principal's desk and sat down. "You said on the phone that Nita hurt someone, Ms. Savok? Any bones broken?"

Lena Savok was long-torsoed and fortyish, projecting an executive-suite cool with her gray suit, stern look, and thick black hair pulled back into a bun. Her office matched her personality—a ruthlessly organized desk with not so much as a stray pen on the blotter, nothing on the walls but diplomas, credentials, and a framed color photograph of a band of musk oxen circled up on the tundra, horns out.

The principal took off her glasses and folded her hands in front of her.

"Mr. and Mrs. Active, I appreciate you coming in. Thankfully, the other student was not seriously injured, just a bloody nose. Her mother took her home."

"What happened?" Grace twisted the fingers of one hand in the other.

"I think it would be best if Nita owns her actions by explaining the situation herself."

Grace pushed back her chair and turned to face Active and Nita. "Well?"

Active got a box of Kleenex from the principal's desk and handed it to Nita, who was back in her chair now. He sat down beside her. She blew her nose loudly, wadded up the Kleenex, and stared at her hands, not saying a word.

Active stroked her shoulder. "It'll be okay, kiddo. Tell us about it."

Nita drew a deep breath and blurted out, "I punched Mindy Harper."

"Why would you do that?" Grace almost shouted.

Nita glared at her. "Because of what she said about you."

Grace's eyes widened and she pressed her hand over her heart. "About me?" She looked like a fox in a trap. Active felt a tremor in his chest.

"Wha—what . . ." Grace's fists were clenched, but not enough to control the trembling.

Active realized he was standing now. "What did Mindy say, Nita?"

The girl's eyes swung from Active to Grace and back again.

He smiled and nodded. "Go ahead, sweetheart."

Nita looked at her lap again. She drew a deep breath that raised, then lowered her shoulders. "She said you killed my Uncle Jason."

Grace's face contorted. Nita looked up, eyes pleading. "Is that true, Mom?"

Grace's mouth was frozen in a silent cry. Active felt the same, but he put an arm around Nita and pulled her into his shoulder.

"No, Nita, that's not what happened." He hoped his voice sounded more certain than he felt.

Nita straightened and looked into his face. "How did he die? I thought his gun went off when he was cleaning it."

"No, he was shot." Active tried to say it calmly, as he would have to the next of kin after any other killing.

"Who by?"

Active turned to Grace, his eyes asking if he should continue to play this by himself. But she found her voice.

"Your aunt confessed to it."

"Aunt Ida? Why?"

Active touched the girl's shoulder again. "We could talk about this at home, ah?" He glanced at the principal. "Not here."

Savok cleared her throat and stood. "I'll step out and give you some privacy."

As the door clicked shut behind the principal, Nita turned back to Active. "Why would she shoot Uncle Jason?" she asked again.

"*Bunnik*, come here." Grace pulled the girl onto her lap and cradled her like a toddler. She stroked Nita's hair, teasing out the tangles at the ends. "Sweetheart, I grew up in a very troubled family. There are some things that I still don't understand. There are some things you may understand when you're older. And there are some things neither of us will ever understand."

Active leaned forward, hands between his knees. He was on a pitching boat in a storm, unsure exactly how to rescue himself and his family. All he could do was brace for the next wave.

"What happened between your aunt and uncle," Grace continued, "is a secret she took to her grave."

Nita looked up at Grace. "But Mindy said—"

"Nita, honey, every family has troubles. Even Mindy's, I'm sure.

But family troubles should stay in the family, with me and you and your dad. And that's where you go when you hear something bad that you don't understand. You don't take village gossip at face value and hash it out with your fists. Okay?"

Nita nodded. Active put out his hand and she moved beside him again. Grace went to the door and waved the principal in.

"Is there something more you would like to say, Nita?" Savok asked as she returned to her desk.

"I was so angry when Mindy said that about Mom." Nita's eyes flashed. "I called her a liar."

"And that's when you hit her?"

Nita touched her cheek. "No, that's when she scratched my face. Then I punched her."

"Ah," the principal said.

"That sounds like a mutual altercation, Ms. Savok," Active said. "With mutual provocation."

"Fair point. But we can't tolerate violence in our school."

"Absolutely not." Active matched the principal's stern tone.

"There must be consequences, no matter who struck the first blow."

"Absolutely," Grace said.

"I think a three-day suspension would be appropriate."

"For both parties, yes, that would fair," Active said.

Savok nodded.

Active stood and extended his hands to Nita and Grace.

The principal picked up a folder and handed it to Nita. "Here is your homework for the rest of the week. I trust we will see you back in school on Monday ready to make better choices and make this a great year."

"Yes, ma'am," Nita said.

Active took Grace's arm and led her and Nita out to the Tahoe. The girl climbed into the back seat, slammed the door, put in earbuds, and buried her face in her phone.

"Nathan, Nathan," Grace said as she crumpled into his arms. "I don't know if I can do it. I mean, the thought of putting another child, and myself, through all of this again in a few years, it just seems so hard, I . . ."

And here they were again. Maybe he'd been fooling himself. Maybe she'd never be ready to have his child. But she was the one who had lived through the destruction wrought by Jason Palmer, was still living through it.

He stroked the back of her head. "I know, baby," he said. "I know."

"I'm so sorry."

"It's your decision." He had to take a deep breath to get the next words out. "If you do choose to have the abortion, do you want me there?"

There was a long silence. "I'm not sure."

CHAPTER FOURTEEN

• *Friday, August 26* •

DEPARTMENT OF PUBLIC SAFETY, CHUKCHI

Lucy Brophy, the Public Safety office manager, stood in front of Active's office door, arms crossed, jaw set, blocking his way in.

"Hey Lucy, what's going on?" He used the most neutral voice he could muster. Things inevitably got touchy from time to time when you worked in close quarters with an ex-girlfriend, especially when the breakup hadn't exactly been symmetrical. And even more so if she came with the job and you were her boss.

He eased around her and motioned her in. She shut the door and took a seat at his desk.

"Damn payroll is messed up again," she said. "Still some bugs in the new software."

"Never trust an upgrade," he said. "Am I right?

She huffed and stared at him.

"How serious is it?" he asked after a few seconds. "Do we need to get Sonny in here?"

Active's half brother was the department's unpaid IT consultant, and much better at it, not to mention faster, than the company that supposedly serviced their network remotely from Anchorage.

"Checks are going to be late again. *Arii*, everybody's gonna yell at me, same like always." Her eyes dared him to say anything. "I'm doing the best I can, okay?"

"Nobody said you weren't, but you could have just sent an email. You didn't need to come in and—"

Tears glistened in the corners of her eyes. So this wasn't about payroll. She had been out for most of the previous week with an unspecified health issue.

"Um, if you need more medical leave . . ."

Now the tears spilled down her cheeks and her underlip began to quiver. She wiped her face with the backs of her hands and smeared lipstick onto her cheek. It looked like a fresh wound. "Do I look all right?"

He decided there was no good answer to that. He passed her a handkerchief. She grabbed it, sopped the wetness from her eyes and cheeks, blew her nose into it, and held it out to him.

He put up his hands. "That's okay."

She stuffed it into a pocket and said nothing.

"What's going—"

"When were you gonna to tell me?"

A wave of confusion rolled over him, and then it clicked. He took a deep breath and slowly let it out. "I'm sorry, Lucy. We haven't told many—"

"Ha! Everybody knows. Everybody but me, apparently."

He shifted in his seat. The lower lip was quivering again. He sensed another burst of tears coming.

"I didn't mean for you to find out that way."

Her hands began to shake, then her shoulders.

"Look, I—can I get you a cup of tea?"

"Tea isn't gonna fix this."

"What, ah, what—"

"I can't . . . I can't . . ." Her face contorted. "I can't have any more babies. I had a hysterectomy."

Active tried to think of something to say, but came up empty. She drew the soggy handkerchief from her pocket, applied it to her nose and eyes again, and hung her head. Her chin bounced off her chest as she sobbed.

Again he searched for something to say or do. Finally, he managed, "Lucy, you and Dan have two great kids."

"You don't get it," she said between sobs. "But how could you? You men always think your parts are so important and ours don't matter."

Active sat back and held his tongue. Nothing for it now but to ride it out.

"How would you feel if all your reproductive organs got cut out?"

He winced.

"Would you still feel like a man? Well, how do you think I feel with all my woman stuff gone?"

Active gritted his teeth. She didn't deserve to hurt like this, and the last thing he wanted was to make it worse. "Lucy, I don't think you're any less a woman, and I'm sure Dan doesn't either."

She rolled her eyes and sniffled.

"And you have a wonderful family, even without any more children."

She twisted the handkerchief and shrugged. "It's not like we wanted a big family like they had around here early days ago. But now it's not even a possibility, you know?"

He nodded, hoping he looked like he actually did know.

"I'll never have another baby with Dan." She paused and her eyes filled as she stared at him. "And I can never have a baby with . . ."

Active's mouth dropped open. "But, Lucy, we haven't—I mean, it's been years, why would you think—"

"I used to dream about it all the time when we were together." A faraway look spread over her face. "He would have your smile and my eyes."

"Lucy, you have to let this go, this conversation isn't app—"

Her eyes snapped back to his. "At least you got to have your dream come true." Her sudden smile seemed forced. "And I'm happy for you. And Gracie." She sniffed loudly and wiped her nose again. "Took you long enough."

Active's phone buzzed and he checked the caller ID. "It's Georgeanne from the ME's office. I have to take this."

He thought he heard her swear under her breath. The feet of her chair screeched as she shoved it back.

Active tapped up the call and asked Georgeanne to hold for a minute. "Lucy, if you do need some more time off, it's not a prob—"

"I'm fine," she growled. "I've got work to do. Who's gonna do it if I don't?" She threw the sodden handkerchief onto his desk and marched out, shoving past Kavik as he entered with a grin.

"Again?" he said. "You two oughta sell tickets. What is it this time?"

Active shook his head, motioned Kavik into a seat, and put the phone on speaker. "Hey, Georgeanne, Chief Active. You got something for us?"

"Mr. Apok's blood alcohol was point-four-five."

Active pushed back in his chair and exhaled. "Over five times the legal limit? You couldn't be mistaken? I did ask you to rush this."

"No mistake. It's why they pay me the big bucks. Like I told you, we're having a body drought right now, and three suspicious deaths in two months in a village of three thousand is kind of an attention-getter."

"Thanks for the fast work, Georgeanne. I owe you. Next time I'm in Anchorage, I'm absolutely gonna buy you the surf and turf at Club Paris, I swear."

"Worst offer I've had all day," Georgeanne said with a grin in her voice. "But your guy—"

"Yeah, could somebody with that much liquor in his system work a rifle under his chin and pull the trigger?"

"Maybe if his name was Lazarus. Mr. Apok was nearly coma-tose. Dead drunk, in layman's terms."

"So assuming the cause of death is a gunshot through the head, someone else besides Jesse Apok pulled the trigger?"

"The cause is, and someone else did, Chief."

Kavik picked up a photograph of Apok's rifle and studied it for a moment. "Any fingerprints on the weapon?"

"Only Mr. Apok's."

"And the cell phone?" Active asked.

"Nothing. But I did find something else a little odd. Contusions on the trigger finger, top and bottom."

"I don't remember seeing anything like that when I—"

"You wouldn't," Georgeanne said. "Not with the naked eye. But I've got all kinds of handy-dandy magnifying tools at my disposal."

"Contusions, huh? Meaning what?"

"Meaning somebody pressed Mr. Apok's finger against the

trigger hard to make the gun go off and he bruised it in the process."

"He couldn't have done it himself?" Active asked.

"Don't think so. Your boy had help."

"Can you lift prints off the finger?"

"Not likely, but I'll see what I can do. Week or so work for you?"

"Yeah. Thanks, Georgeanne."

Kavik slapped his knee, splashed coffee onto his pants. "So. It was homicide."

"Looks like."

"Do we pick up Monique Rogers now?"

"Let's run it down first," Active said.

Kavik ticked off the points on his fingers. "She had the motive to get rid of Todd—so that Evie couldn't have him. And she had access to the murder weapon—those weather balloons."

"And she knew Jesse—the person who had access to the fuel tanks and the opportunity to put in the balloons," Active said.

Kavik nodded. "So she could have blackmailed him into help-ing her because she knew his drinking on the job could get him fired, and then he wouldn't be able to pay his child support—which is clearly leverage for the ex-girlfriend to keep him from seeing his son."

"And once I talked to her the first time, she thinks maybe she's under suspicion and—"

"And if she found out we talked to Jesse, too," Kavik said, "then she had motive to get rid of the only person who could rat her out."

"Long chain of assumptions," Active said. "She planned this, knew he had a rifle, knew how to load it, all of that."

Kavik took a long swig of coffee. "I think she took advantage of the situation more than planning it. Jesse talked about hunting at work. His place isn't that big. If she looked around, she'd find the rifle. Her dad was in the military, probably had guns around the house. And she is half village girl, don't forget. She'd know how to shoot."

"Setting him up with the gun under his chin would be the easy part. How does she get to that point?"

Kavik crossed the room to refill his coffee cup, speaking as he went and returned. "She comes to his place, she's frantic to talk to him. Maybe she tells him we've questioned her, and she's scared. She wants to make sure they have their alibis straight."

"He's already drunk, confused, the guilt is eating at him," Active said. "Maybe they argue about what to do."

"Yeah," Kavik said. "The voices the neighbor and Denise heard. She pushes him to drink some more to calm down. Then, at some point soon after, he passes out at the kitchen table."

"She takes a minute to think, decides Jesse's gonna crack eventually, and sees an easy way out."

"So he's deadweight, slumped over the table. It'd be hard to maneuver a rifle between his knees and under his chin unless she dragged him back in his chair."

"But she's athletic," Active said. "In great shape from all the running, and he's not that heavy—wait, where's that picture of the feet?"

He shuffled through the photos and turned up a shot from a low angle, showing not much more than the bottoms of Apok's bare feet framed by the underside of the table and one of its legs.

"Here." Active pointed at the lower corner of the photo and shoved it across the desk.

Kavik squinted at the image. "What am I looking at?"

Active tapped a spot on the photo. "This light area here on the floor? Next to the bottom of the table leg? See how the floor is darker around it?"

Kavik nodded. "Sure, the table leg was covering that spot. Oh, yeah—she moved the table, not the chair with him in it. That would be easier, all right."

"Now we have the opportunity, the motive, and the weapon. But only Jesse's prints are on the gun."

"She could've covered hers up by putting Jesse's hands around the rifle."

"Yep. And no prints on the flip phone," Active said.

"Too bad it was an older one you don't swipe to unlock."

Active studied his notes. "No physical evidence, no witnesses. How do we place Monique at Jesse's apartment?"

"If it went down around nine that morning, she had plenty of time before her day shift started to go to his apartment and then get to work before we showed up to talk to her around eleven."

"But nobody saw her or a purple Jeep near the Pamiuktuk that morning."

"Nope." Kavik leaned back in his chair. "Huh."

"Alan Long talked to all the neighbors?"

"Yeah, all of—no, wait, there was one he missed. Guy named Lester Anderson."

"And why was that?"

"He was already at work when Alan arrived. Then he went in for gallbladder surgery the next day. He's been recuperating at home, not feeling too great. Long was giving him three, four days before he questioned him."

"Three or four days? That'd make it almost a week since Apok died. Monique Rogers is coming to the end of her two-week rotation. She could be on a plane to California, or who knows, maybe

Dubai, if we don't act fast." Active raked the photos into a stack and dropped them into a padded envelope. "Let's bring her in now, with or without her cooperation."

"Do we have enough?" Kavik asked.

"Not yet." Active headed for the door, slipping into his jacket on the way. "You go to Mr. Anderson's place, give him a quick apology for the intrusion, find out if he saw anything that puts Ms. Rogers at the murder scene, and get back here as soon as possible."

Monique Rogers sat on a metal chair in the same room where Jesse Apok had been questioned four days earlier. She had that look suspects always got, shaking on the inside, cool on the outside.

"What is this about, Chief?" It came out casual, but her voice quavered a little and she gripped the edge of the table a little too hard.

Active gave her a few more seconds to stew, then dropped the envelope of photos from Apok's apartment on the table. He pulled another picture out of his shirt pocket and laid it on top of the envelope.

Monique stared at the photo of Apok and his son from the dead man's refrigerator, then at Active.

"Jesse Apok. So?"

Active slid the photo closer to her. "That's Corey with him. Three years old, told me how much he likes to go fishing with his daddy."

Monique leaned over for another look. "I see the resemblance. But, again, Chief: So?" She pushed the photo back toward him.

"Yes, Corey does look like his daddy." Active tapped the photo. "A father-son fishing trip. Good times, ah?"

Monique didn't respond.

Active opened the envelope and fanned out the photos of Jesse Apok with the top of his head missing. "But now, not so much."

She looked, flinched, and turned away. "What are you trying to do, scare me to death? These are horrible."

"I just thought you might want some souvenirs of your handiwork."

Monique covered her heart with both hands, eyes wide. "You think *I* did that? You're crazy. I would never—you can't think—I wouldn't have any reason to do such a terrible thing!"

She shoved the photos back across the table. "And I heard he committed suicide, anyway."

"We're talking homicide, here, Ms. Rogers, not suicide." Active paused to let it sink in. She kept her game face on, except for a little twitch in the left eyebrow. "But maybe we can straighten this out. Where were you between eight and ten A.M. on August twenty-third?"

"Um, let me—three days ago? Tuesday? At work. Which you very well know. You and that other officer were there, remember?"

"That was around eleven. Jesse died around nine. Can you account for your whereabouts at that time?"

"Really, Chief, is this necessary—"

"Your whereabouts, Ms. Rogers? Between eight and ten A.M., August twenty-third?"

"I was at work, like I said. I logged onto my computer around seven-forty-five, same as always."

"Sure. But you had plenty of time to leave and come back. Anyone see you there?"

"No, it's a solitary job. But the computer automatically logs out after fifteen minutes if I don't stay on it."

"Wasn't that the day you had computer problems?"

"Oh, yeah." She studied her fingernails. "That does kind of complicate things, I guess." She pushed at the photos again. "Can you put these away? They're very upsetting."

Active studied her shaking shoulders and the way she pressed her lips together. All that distress—real, or just a good performance?

"You weren't upset when you were shoving that rifle under Jesse's chin. You must have been cool as ice to set it up like a suicide like you did. Of course, him being passed out drunk, that had to help."

Monique's eyes bounced from side to side. Was that a tear forming in the corner of one?

"But . . . but why would I want to kill Jesse?"

"Because Jesse's conscience was getting the better of him. He was about to confess to helping you kill Evie Kavoonah and Todd Brenner. So you shut him up and made it look like a village suicide."

She half stood, flung out her arms and shouted. "Todd and Evie, too? That's insane!"

Active spread his hands. "Sit down, Ms. Rogers. We're not done here."

She slumped back into the chair and crossed her arms. "Fine. Get all your crazy accusations out so I can tell you how ridiculous they are and leave this place."

He leaned forward and narrowed his eyes. "Evie was pregnant. Did you know that? There was another life on that plane that never even had a chance to start."

"I see. So this is where I'm supposed to cave in from guilt?" She tried to laugh, but it came out halfway between a cough and a sob. "I didn't do anything wrong, so I don't have anything to feel guilty about. Think about it, Chief. Why would I want to kill Evie and Todd? They were actually kind of a cute couple."

He doodled in his notebook. A face resembling Nita's took shape under his pen. He put the pen in his shirt pocket.

"Maybe you only wanted to kill one of them. Like Todd, maybe. He dumped you for another woman. That had to hurt."

Her face said it did, but her mouth said, "I already told you, I moved on. Sounds like I lucked out. I'm not looking to be some man's baby factory."

She shifted in her seat and paused for a few seconds. Her face softened. "Don't get me wrong. I am sorry to hear about Evie and Todd and the baby. And if somebody crashed that plane, that's awful, and I hope you catch them. But even if I had a reason to, how can you think I brought down that plane when I don't even know how they work?"

"But you did know the person who fueled that plane. So maybe you and Jesse cooked up a plan to make sure it would run out of fuel at exactly the wrong time."

Monique studied her nails. "You've got quite an imagination, Chief. I somehow got Jesse to sabotage the plane? What did I promise him—his own weather balloon?"

"You knew about his bottle; that was your leverage. You had the power to get him fired. And even if he got caught and tried to lay it on you, who's gonna believe a village drunk, right?" Active stood up and tossed his pen onto the notebook. He squared his shoulders. "I can prove you killed Jesse, and the dominoes will come tumbling down against you in the murders of Evie and Todd."

She was turning the crime-scene photos face down, one by

one. "Really?" Her eyes smoldered as she looked up. "You can't prove I was anywhere near Jesse's place when he died. Because I wasn't. And you can't show I had anything to do with that plane. Because I didn't." Monique stood up, her cool back in place. "I'll be going now, Chief. As I've said before, good luck with your investigation."

A knock sounded at the door and Kavik poked his head in. "A moment, Chief?"

"Wait, please, Ms. Rogers. I'll be right back."

Monique rolled her eyes and crossed her arms as Active stepped out and shut the door.

"What have you got?"

"I talked to Anderson."

"The gallbladder guy," Active said.

Kavik raised his eyebrows, yes. "He saw a Jeep parked half a block down the street from Apok's place around eight that morning. He passed it on his way to work, said he always slows down on that part of the road because of the big pothole. He saw a woman in the driver's seat. No description though."

"A purple Jeep?"

"He could only say it was a dark color, but it definitely had the word 'Wrangler' on the side."

"That'll do. Come with me."

Monique turned to the door of the interrogation room as the two officers entered. "Hands behind your back, Ms. Rogers," Active said.

"I'm getting the hell out of here," she shouted. She tried to slide around him.

Active caught her elbow, whirled her around and locked a cuff onto one wrist, then the other.

"Monique Rogers, you're under arrest for the murders of Jesse Apok, Evie Kavoonah, and Todd Brenner. You have the right to remain si—"

The rest of the Miranda warning was drowned out by a storm of profanity.

CHAPTER FIFTEEN

• *Saturday, August 27* •

DISTRICT ATTORNEY'S OFFICE, CHUKCHI

"There's no point bringing charges if I can't sell it at trial." District Attorney Theresa Procopio tossed the Monique Rogers file across her desk with such force that it nearly slid onto Active's lap. "For this you dragged me in on a weekend? A weather balloon and a dark-colored Jeep? That's it?"

"So far," Active said. "We're still working it."

A four-wheeler backfired as it sputtered past Procopio's first-floor office window in the building that housed the court system and the Alaska Department of Law. Like most other big buildings in the Arctic, it perched on wooden pilings to avoid melting the permafrost underneath and being swallowed up in the resulting mud. The shriveled blossoms of dead flowers nodded in the wind from a window box.

Procopio rattled her nails on the desktop and arched an eyebrow beneath her curly brown mane.

The nails were candy-apple red, Active noticed, a marked departure from Procopio's normal disdain for ornamentation. And she seemed a little trimmer lately. Had she shed a few of the pounds that had accumulated since her arrival in Chukchi several years back? There was even a trace of the fresh-faced public defender who had begun her village legal career in a most un-village suit jacket and skirt. Could there be a man in Theresa Procopio's life after all this time?

Or a woman? Active realized he still didn't know.

"Details?" The nails clattered on the desk again.

He pulled himself back to the Two-Five-Mike case, as he had come to think of it.

"We went over her Jeep with a fine-tooth comb this morning. Not a trace of blood or anything else of interest. Turns out it's a rental from Tundra. She took it in on Thursday for a scheduled service, which came with a wash, and she also had them detail it, which she had to pay for herself."

"Detailed? In Chukchi? Seriously?" Procopio pulled back the file and looked at her notes. "And Thursday was, what, two days after the murder? So she wanted to get rid of something?"

Active sighed. "Or she likes a really clean car. The kid at Tundra said she always has it washed and detailed once a month, which he had never even heard of till she explained it to him. And her room at the Shore Inn is probably the cleanest place in Chukchi. Not a spoon in the sink, clothes fresh from the washer. Like an operating room in there, you could eat off the floor."

"How about her computer and phone?"

Active shook his head. "They weren't password-protected, but we've struck out so far."

"No texts to or from Apok the day of the murder?"

Active shook his head. "Or any other day. No communication

between them at all, as far as we can tell. A lot of texts back and forth with her cousin Dora about Lienhofer and the great and small of male genitalia."

"You guys would be surprised what we talk about when you're not around."

Active shrugged. "Not if your wife makes you watch enough chick flicks."

"But seriously, no mention of our murder victims in those texts? By name or implication?"

"No. The Lienhofer stuff is mostly about the owner, Delilah. I don't think I've ever seen the B-word used so many times in a single sentence."

"Millennials using sentences? When did that start?"

Active smiled. Procopio didn't.

"Danny Kavik is still going through the emails on her laptop," he said. "But we're not optimistic. Turns out it's synced with her phone, which we already went through. So we don't expect much unless we get lucky with her internet search history."

"Let's make sure we nail down what little we do have," Procopio said. "I want to know about every Jeep Wrangler in town."

Active nodded. "Alan Long is working that."

"You search the weather station yet?"

"We're on it."

"What's that mean?"

"Local law enforcement can't just walk into a federal facility and confiscate property without permission. The weather bureau will give it to us, but, you know, it's a bureaucracy. The paperwork was supposed to be faxed over this morning. We've made a couple phone calls, it'll probably take a couple more. The usual."

"You've got to be kidding. Let the feds muck this up after they already concluded a double murder was an aviation accident? I'll make a call, the fax will be waiting when you get back to your office."

"Really? You know a guy?"

"I might." A smile softened the district attorney's all-business facade. Was there perhaps even a slight flutter of the eyelashes? "This FBI agent in Anchorage."

"Uh-huh."

"Shut up." She brushed her hair out of her eyes. The unruly curls immediately flopped forward again. "A woman has needs."

The backfiring four-wheeler chugged past the window again, this time in the opposite direction.

"Now, if we could focus here?" Procopio straightened up, all business again. "Our case against Monique is weak on the Kavoonah-Brenner homicides. And if we're going with eliminating a witness as her motive for killing Apok, we need more on the first crime to make the second one stick. You're thinking love gone wrong was behind it all?"

"Oldest motive in the book. But, yeah, we've got some blanks to fill in, and we're getting close to the twenty-four-hour mark—"

"When you have to release her if I can't bring charges." Procopio glanced at the clock. "Four hours and counting." Her fingernails rattled on the desk again.

Danny Kavik gazed up at the domed ceiling of the weather station garage like a kid at a planetarium. A Nikon DSLR hung from a strap around his neck. "You could almost fit an airplane in here."

"Or plan how to bring one down." Active pulled a rubbery white roll off a shelf in the tall metal cabinet, carried it to the table in the middle of the room, and unfurled it next to the spread-out balloon that he and Cowboy had retrieved from the tank in the right wing of Two-Five-Mike.

"Same size, same color," Kavik said. He circled the table with his Nikon.

"It feels a little different, though." Active ran a fingertip over the latex of the weather-service balloon. "Not quite as smooth as ours."

"Ours was in a gas tank for, like, six weeks," Kavik said.

"Good point. But I still wonder if there was some variation between different batches, different suppliers, that kind of thing. I'm gonna check a few of the others. You search the office, ah?"

"On it." Kavik headed for the side door. "Anything specific we're looking for?"

"Any sign of communication between Monique and Jesse—phone number, address on a scrap of paper, anything to show they were in touch. Be sure to check the trash can and the phone messages."

Active began pulling rolled-up balloons out of the cabinet. Eight of the deflated spheres were spread and stacked on the table when Kavik returned with a half-full trash bag.

"How's it going, Chief?"

Active shook his head. "Slow and inconclusive. You?"

"Not much. Voicemails on her phone go back only two days, one from her supervisor and three from the IT guy in Fairbanks. Work stuff mostly, except the IT guy seems a little friendly. He calls her 'Brown Sugar.'"

"Whoa."

"A braver man than I," Kavik said as he emptied the trash bag onto the table. Two pairs of brightly colored running shoes, five bottles of vitamins and diet supplements, three protein bars, a carton of vanilla soy milk, and a bottle of something labeled "black cohosh." Kavik picked it up and studied the label.

"Black cohosh?" Active said.

"Supposed to control PMS, apparently."

"I'd say she's wasting her money."

"And other symptoms of hormonal imbalance," Kavik went on. "Like hot flashes."

"Huh," Active said. "Which I suppose could explain why she was wearing the anorak and then drinking that cold Diet Pepsi when we talked to her the morning Jesse was killed."

Kavik nodded. "Rather than having just come back from killing him. Which means we have even less reason to hold her."

Kavik's cell phone pinged. "Ah. It's the vehicle information from Long." Kavik tapped the phone a couple of times, then scrolled down and pinch-zoomed. "*Arii,* as both my *aanas* would say."

"Not good?"

"Turns out, there are three Jeep Wranglers in Chukchi. One is white, so we can scratch it. Of the other two, one is purple, one is dark blue."

"Purple is Monique, obviously. And the blue one?"

Kavik shook his head. "Denise Sheldon."

"*Arii* is right. She already told us she was there that morning."

"Maybe we should talk to her again?"

"Her and Apok, a crime of passion might make sense. But a premeditated killing? You saw how she was with that kid. I can't see her taking Corey to a murder and leaving him in the car while she does it."

Active's cell phone chimed and the caller ID for the Anchorage crime lab came up. He showed Kavik and put the phone on speaker.

"What do you have for me, Kalani?" he asked Georgeanne's assistant.

"Hey, Chief. First time I ever analyzed a balloon as evidence." The deep rumble of the Hawaiian's voice rattled Active's phone.

"Can you tell where it came from?"

"Sorry, yeah. I put a black light on it, and there's a row of triangles along the neck you can't see in regular light that identify the manufacturer. Outfit in Wisconsin called Rugged-Line. But they distribute to retailers all over the country and on the internet. No way to tell where yours was bought."

"But it is a weather balloon."

"Nope. Same size, but this type of balloon is mostly used by hobbyists. It's neoprene."

"Not latex?" Active asked with a sinking feeling.

"Nope, definitely not latex. The weather people use latex balloons because they're more flexible, they can stand up to more wind. But you gonna put one in a fuel tank, neoprene is mo' bettah." Active remembered from past conversations that Kalani's Hawaiian pidgin came out when he had a big discovery to divulge.

"Why's that?"

"Neoprene is used to make fuel lines 'cause it's impervious to the stuff. But latex, you put that in gasoline, it's gonna dissolve on you like toilet papuh."

Active tapped out of the call and stared at the balloons spread out on the table.

"If it's not a weather balloon, we have no connection between the murder weapon and Monique," Active said.

"She could have gotten hold of a neoprene balloon," Kavik said with an utter lack of conviction.

"So could anyone else in Chukchi."

They continued to study the balloons in silence. Active rubbed the balloon from Two-Five-Mike, then one of Monique's balloons.

Kavik followed suit. "We gotta cut her loose, don't we?"

"We do," Active said. "But she's not totally off the hook."

"Right. She did have a motive to bring down that plane. And she did have a connection to the person who had access to the fuel tank the night before it went down."

"It all comes back to Jesse Apok."

CHAPTER SIXTEEN

• *Monday, August 29* •

E-Z MARKET, CHUKCHI

Esther Noyakuk sat on a green and white lawn chair with her feet propped up on a plastic milk crate outside the back door of the E-Z Market.

"Diabetes," she told Active and Kavik as they pulled up a couple of crates for makeshift seats. "Makes my legs swell."

Esther was mid-fortyish and heavy, with an E-Z Market name tag pinned to her blouse. She took a nervous pull on a straw stuck into a plastic Diet Coke bottle. "First Jesse, now Paul? He said he'll be back Saturday. Is he—"

"No, no, Mrs. Noyakuk." Active realized she must have assumed the worst after his call that morning to say they wanted to talk to her. "We just need to ask your son some questions about Jesse, that's all. Anything he could tell us about any trouble Jesse was in, why he might have done what he did."

The woman pressed the sleeve of her blouse to her

sweat-dampened forehead. "My blood pressure is not so good anymore." She forced a weak smile, took another sip of soda, and wrinkled her nose. "*Arii,* this diet stuff tastes like nothing."

"Paul's only two days late," Active said. "Maybe he didn't catch any caribou and wants to stay in camp longer. That's pretty normal, ah?"

"Not two days, not with Paul. He always plan. He's never 'All of a sudden I'll do this.' I worry so much about him since he come back from Iraq this spring. Before he's always funny—joking, talking with everybody all the time. Now he's quiet, like he's depressed. He doesn't sleep. He has nightmares. He stays with me and I hear him yelling in the middle of the night. He's supposed to take medication, all right, but . . ."

"Nightmares about Iraq?"

Esther raised her eyebrows, yes. "Maybe that never happen if I have money to send him to college. He's so smart. He knows everything about computers and phones and stuff. Other kids, they get in trouble at school for fighting. My Paul, only time ever he get in trouble is when he correct his teachers because he know more than them."

"Did he talk to you about the nightmares?"

"No. I never think he talk to nobody about that, not even Jesse. He holds it all in." She slapped her stomach. "That's not good, ah? Rot you from the inside."

"How has he been lately? Did he seem particularly upset about anything?"

"He talk more about that little girl sometimes."

"What little girl?"

"The one die last winter before he come back. He's always like, 'Why did she die? She didn't have to die.'"

"And was she—"

"I keep telling him all these years, that's not his daughter. He's only seventeen when she's born, still a kid in high school. That woman go with so many men, I bet she don't even know which one is the father. But Paul, he never listen to me. Nobody ever listen to me."

"Who is this woman?"

Esther spat on the ground beside her chair. "*Arii*, an un-Christian name, that girl. Loralei. She got that blue hair, tattoos, come in the store sometimes, get that energy drink hype you up or a candy bar. How she live on that stuff?"

"Do you know the little girl's name?"

Esther shook her head, spat again. "Something off of one of those candy bars. *Arii*, what—Hershey, that's it. What kind of name is that for a baby?"

"She was how old?" Active asked.

"Six last March, then all of sudden, she die."

"What happened to her?"

"Who knows? Her mother probably never take care of her right way. Woman like that don't care nothing about no kids." She wiped her forehead again, then pressed the tissue against the beads of moisture on her upper lip. "Maybe they're smart ones, not worry about their kids all the time."

"Do you need water? Danny could get some."

The woman nodded, closed her eyes, and exhaled. "That would be nice, young man."

Kavik rose and went into E-Z Market.

"Do you think Paul would harm himself?" Active asked.

Esther patted her chest. "I don't know what he's thinking no more. Why does he all of a sudden go off hunting and not come back when he say? First Jesse, now, Paul? I already have to go to one funeral."

Kavik returned with a bottle of water. Esther uncapped it and drank, with a nod of thanks.

"Does he know about Jesse's death?"

"No. He was already gone."

"Are you sure?"

Esther raised her eyebrows, yes. "I drive him down where he got his boat tied up. He load in his gear and start out across the bay and then he turn around and wave at me. The sun, it was just come up and it hit his face, he look like my little boy again. Almost make me cry, and I say a prayer for him. Then I take the four-wheeler back over here for work."

"What time was this?"

"Around six-thirty. I have to open the store at seven, Tuesday mornings."

Active looked up from his notebook. "Six-thirty Tuesday? So that was before—"

"Ah-hah," Esther said with a nod. "Before anyone know about Jesse kill himself, otherwise Paul would never go. I should have said a prayer for him, too, poor Jesse."

She took another sip of water and looked at her watch. "My break time's over, all right."

She labored up from the chair. Active stood and put out an arm. She clutched it with both hands and looked at him with a plea in her eyes. "Can you go out there, see if he's all right?"

"Yes, ma'am. We'll fly out there first thing tomorrow. Do you know where he camps?"

"He always hunt around what they call Ivisuk. You know that place?"

"I know it," Kavik said. "My family goes up there, too. Caribou are lots and good at Ivisuk this time of year, all right."

CHAPTER SEVENTEEN

• *Tuesday, August 30* •

EN ROUTE TO IVISUK

Cowboy's new Cessna 185 roared off the float pond into a late summer dawn, blue and crisp. As they climbed away from the airport, a west wind scuffed up whitecaps on the gray slate of Chukchi Bay.

"Ivisuk?" Active asked through the intercom as Cowboy throttled back, leveled off, and swung the plane northwest toward the mouth of the Katonak River. "Why do they call it that?"

"I don't know," Kavik said from the back seat. "People just do."

Active studied the terrain ahead. The Katonak crawled away from the coast for a few miles, then twisted through the Sulana Hills and crossed the Katonak Flats toward the Brooks Range.

"Still big," Cowboy said.

As usual, his thoughts seemed to track Active's. "Still empty."

Cowboy pointed over the nose. "Ivisuk Creek comes into the Katonak over there where the foothills start on the far side of the Flats. Can't land in the creek, too rocky and shallow, so I drop people on a little lake about a half mile in. You oughta be able to walk to his camp from there."

"Assuming we find it." Active studied his notebook. "He's in an aluminum boat, one of those drop fronts, like a small landing craft. Big red Evinrude outboard, little canvas wheelhouse, with a Yamaha four-wheeler on board. And he uses a white wall tent."

"And probably caribou hides to sleep on," Kavik put in from the back seat. "Standard Eskimo hunting camp."

"I thought we weren't allowed to say the E-word anymore," Cowboy said.

Active looked to see if the pilot was grinning under his headset. He was.

"Does he mean 'Eskimo'?" Kavik asked.

"Of course he does," Active said.

"That's right," Cowboy said. "The feds banned it, is what I heard."

This rang a bell with Active. He fished through his memory for the details, then it came to him. "Ah, no, they didn't ban it exactly, they're just not going to use it themselves anymore. Like in laws and regulations. They have to say 'Alaska Native' now."

Kavik snorted from the back seat. "And what if the Alaska Native happens to be an Eskimo?"

"Don't blame me," Active said. "I wasn't consulted."

"Just don't call my Grampa Billy a Native," Kavik said. "When he was a young buck working the canneries in Southeast, some of the restaurants still had those signs that said, 'No dogs, no Natives.'"

"Which would include Eskimos," Cowboy said. "Right?"

"Maybe, but it's not the same," Kavik said. "At least they didn't put it on the signs. Anyway, the canneries liked Eskimos. They were smarter than Filipinos, according to Billy. And they worked harder, too."

They droned along in silence for a while. The north shore of Chukchi Bay passed beneath the wings, then the Sulana Hills.

Cowboy spoke again. This time Active could hear the grin in his voice.

"How about Inuit, then? That's what the *naluaqmiut* backpackers call you guys, Inuit. Couple days ago, I dropped some kayakers way up on the Katonak, and one of the girls was just raving about how cool it was to see you Inuits up close and personal."

"She oughta meet Billy," Kavik said. "Inuit's a Canadian word, and, as he would happily tell her, 'I ain't no fucking Canadian. I'm an American and I'm an Eskimo, American Inupiat Eskimo, goddammit, and don't call me no fucking Inuit.'"

"I like your grandfather," Active said.

"So," Cowboy said. "Inupiat is okay then?"

"Always," Kavik said.

"And Eskimo? I can still call you Eskimo too?"

"What do you think, Nathan?" Kavik asked.

Active put a grin in his own voice. "Once in a while. But don't push it, *naluaqmiu.*"

Cowboy just grunted.

They rumbled on across the Katonak Flats, and the foothills around the mouth of the Ivisuk grew in the windshield.

"So, Paul," Cowboy said over the headset. "He gonna be trouble?"

"Just a person of interest."

"For what?"

"Police business, Cowboy."

"What police business?"

"Do we have to go through this again?"

"Like I can't guess. We bringing him back?"

"Not that we know of. I'll call you on the satphone when we're done."

Active and Kavik were about a half mile from the lake where Cowboy had set down the 185, thrashing their way through a big patch of alders.

At least, Active reflected, mosquito season was past its peak with fall coming on, so this trek was nothing like the climb up the ridge above the Hawk River. Today, they didn't even need DEET.

They came out of the alders and there, a quarter mile ahead, lay the camp they had seen from the air. A white wall tent poked up from a gentle rise, like a shard of ice on the gold-brown tundra that rolled away to a wall of gray and tan hills. Beyond, snow-covered peaks loomed blue and hazy in the early light.

There was no sign of Noyakuk, not from this side, but a Yamaha four-wheeler was parked beside the tent. Active thought he caught the tang of blood and perhaps fresh caribou meat under the scent of an overnight rain. He motioned to Kavik, they circled around to the front of the tent. And there was Noyakuk.

He sat in profile, legs splayed out in a wide V. His chin on his chest, the lower half of his face obscured by a heavy camo jacket, the Crazy Eskimo ball cap in place.

At his feet on the blue tarp were three field-dressed caribou: backstraps, ribs, front and hindquarters, with the hides spread fur-down on the tundra nearby. A bloodstained wood-and-canvas pack frame leaned against the tent. No heads, antlers, or guts, meaning the kills had been made some distance from camp.

"Paul! Paul Noyakuk!" Active called as they approached.

Noyakuk didn't respond. Was he the next corpse in the case? No: as they stepped closer, Active heard him mumbling.

He did a quick scan for weapons. A rifle laid out on a sleeping bag was visible through the doorway of the tent, stock out. An ammo clip lay near it on the tent floor. Active calculated it would take Noyakuk several seconds to get to the weapon, shove in the clip, work a round into the chamber, and start firing. Assuming, of course, he hadn't left a round in the chamber or another clip in the gun and didn't have a sidearm in his jacket.

On the other hand, there was no reason to suspect Noyakuk was interested in shooting anything but caribou. Whatever the case, he still hadn't moved.

Active waved Kavik around to Noyakuk's side, then unsnapped his holster, eased out his Glock, and held it behind his back as he crouched in front of the hunter. He sensed Kavik unholstering, too, and moving away a couple of paces.

"Paul Noyakuk?" Active said.

Noyakuk's head jerked up and he shouted, "I am the caribou!"

Active jumped back a little and brought the Glock to his side, but Noyakuk's hands remained in his lap and he sat still again.

Active resumed his crouch and studied the hunter. No smell of alcohol, but he had a thousand-yard stare, and his face was smeared with blood.

"I'm Chief Active from Chukchi Public Safety. How you doing, Paul? You okay? Your mom asked us to check on you. Paul?"

"I am the caribou!" Noyakuk repeated, eyes blazing out from the mask of blood.

"He's out of it," Active murmured to Kavik. "You wanna try?"

Kavik dropped to a crouch beside him. "Hey, Paul. It's Danny.

Danny Kavik. We played ball at Chukchi High, remember? You and me and Jesse?"

Noyakuk's eyes swung to Kavik's face. He blinked twice. "What are you doing here?" he asked.

"Your mom sent us. She's worried about you, man."

Noyakuk held Kavik's gaze. "My mother is the caribou."

"Are you hurt, buddy?" Kavik asked.

Noyakuk stared blankly for a couple of seconds, then broke into a grin. The caked blood on his cheeks cracked. "Danny!"

"Yeah, that's right," Kavik said. "It's me, Danny! Listen, I need you to keep your hands in your lap there, okay? I'm going to move closer and check your jacket and your pockets, okay? We don't want you hurting yourself or anyone else."

Kavik patted him down, and came up with chewing gum, a cell phone, and a Kershaw folding knife. He dropped the gum back into the cargo pocket it came from and passed the knife and phone to Active, who stashed them in his jacket pocket.

"Paul, look at me." Noyakuk made eye contact and Kavik went on. "Listen, I'm going to touch your face and head to see where all that blood came from, okay?"

"Blood of my brother, my blood brother, blood of my brother . . ." Noyakuk stared at the tundra between his legs as Kavik examined him.

Kavik turned to Active. "Caribou blood, I'm pretty sure. No sign of injury." He shook his head. "I thought he was with us there for a minute, but—"

"Blood of my brother," Noyakuk said again.

"Your brother, huh?" Kavik unzipped Noyakuk's jacket to check his chest. His clothing was dry, but he'd begun to shiver.

"My brother caribou." Noyakuk pointed into the distance, exposing a scabbed-over scrape on his wrist and knuckles.

Kavik took hold of Noyakuk's sleeve. "What happened here, Paul?"

Noyakuk looked down at his arm and pulled it to his side like a broken wing. "Ah, I fell," he said. "I fell when I was getting out of the boat, all right."

"You're cold, man. Let's make some coffee, ah?"

Active went into the tent, cleared Noyakuk's rifle, pocketed the clip, ran a quick check of the backpack on the floor, and dragged out the sleeping bag. He covered Noyakuk's legs with it while Kavik fired up a camp stove and put on coffee.

"I need a smoke, man," Noyakuk said. Active rummaged through the backpack, found cigarettes and matches, and passed them to Noyakuk.

He lit up with shaky hands and exhaled into the damp air. He wiped some of the blood from around his eyes, and the thousand-yard stare was gone now.

Active crouched in front of him again. "I hear you and Jesse Apok were like brothers."

"Yeah." Noyakuk took another drag and gazed out over the tundra. "But I'm done with all that now."

"Done with Jesse?"

"With Jesse. With the human race."

"The whole human race?"

"The whole motherfucker, man."

"Why's that?"

Kavik handed Noyakuk a cup of steaming coffee. He cradled it against his chest with one hand and took another drag on the cigarette.

"Humans have no souls. The caribou have souls. They take care of their own." Noyakuk sipped from the cup and winced as the coffee hit his mouth. "I am the caribou!" he shouted. The stare was back.

Active glanced at the gray clouds gathering over the hills. More rain was on the way, maybe an early snow. How to get Noyakuk into his right mind before the weather closed in and they got stuck out here for the night, or even several nights? He studied Noyakuk for a few moments and finally noticed the blue patch with wings and a star on the shoulder of his camo jacket.

"Is that Air Force?" He pointed at the insignia.

"Yeah, I was a JTAC in Iraq for a year. Fighting ISIS, man."

"A JTAC is—"

"Joint Terminal Attack Controller. We were set up in operations centers away from the battlefield, watching the video feeds from the drones. We analyzed the data and called in air strikes."

His switch to formal technical speech was jarring, but at least Noyakuk was back for a moment. "Wow," Active said. "How'd you get into that?"

Noyakuk shrugged. "I was always good with computers, all right."

"More like a genius," Kavik broke in. "A regular Mark Zuckerberg."

Noyakuk shrugged again. "I took the test when I enlisted, and they placed me in what they called an 'elite unit.'" He grinned. "Not bad for a dumb Eskimo, ah?"

"I never liked that term much," Active said. "You don't really think we're dumb, do you?"

"Me no savvy, me no know. Me just plain old Eskimo!"

He grinned again, as did Active. It was the default Chukchi comeback for any question too silly to deserve an answer. Like most Inupiat jokes, it was merry and serious at the same time.

"You should be proud. Really proud," Active said.

"It was just a job. Like any other."

"Why didn't you stay in?" Active asked. "Gotta pay better than janitor work, right?"

Noyakuk paused and his mouth tightened. "A janitor don't have to decide who lives or dies."

"But if it's war and it's the enemy . . ."

Noyakuk's eyes lit with a fiery glare. "It's not always the enemy! I showed them the data! I told them it could be a school! I—" He shut down again, looking ahead blankly, chest heaving.

Active gave him some time. Then, "So. You took some time off from work to go hunting?"

"Gotta get back out in the country to clear my head." The techno warrior had vanished and the caribou hunter was back.

"Something been bothering you?"

Noyakuk faced him dead on. "Yeah, like I told you. The human race."

"Does that include Jesse?"

Noyakuk lit another cigarette. "Jesse's a good guy."

"Why didn't he come out here with you?"

"He gotta work."

"When's the last time you saw him?"

"Monday last week, I guess. I go by his place, tell him he oughta *malik* me. He say he's late for work, he gotta go."

Active backtracked and realized that was the same day he and Kavik had questioned Apok. "Did he seem worried about anything? Anyone giving him a hard time?"

"Yeah. He thought Denise will never let him see his boy no more. He was all stressed out, say he can't live without that Corey. I tell him 'Don't do nothing crazy, man.' I tell him, 'I'll bring back a caribou, I'll cook up some ribs, we'll talk about it, we'll figure something out, ah?'"

Noyakuk drew on the cigarette. "Why you asking about Jesse? Did something happen to him?" He glanced at Kavik. "Danny?" His head swiveled to Active, then back to Kavik.

"Paul," Active said, trying to catch Noyakuk's darting eyes, "Jesse is dead."

"No-o-o! Fu-u-uck!"

Noyakuk crumpled. Kavik reached out to grab his shoulder, but was too slow. Noyakuk pitched forward onto the caribou meat, crying and slathering his face with blood.

Kavik pulled him back and hoisted him to his feet. Noyakuk rested his forehead against Kavik's chest, sobbing. When he lifted his head to stand on his own, there were smears of blood and mucus on Kavik's jacket.

"Why he gotta kill himself? He's always talking about that shit when he's drunk, but I never think he'll—why he gotta fucking do that, man?"

Kavik walked Noyakuk to a grassy spot and sat him down, then rejoined Active at the tent.

"Whattaya think?" Kavik asked. "We can't leave him like this."

"We'll take him back with us. I'll call Cowboy and get him back up here." Active pulled out his satphone and powered it up.

The sky was spitting snow by the time he finished the call. Icy needles pricked their cheeks. Noyakuk sat with his head between his knees.

"Might as well start breaking down the camp," Active said. "Noyakuk won't be any help, and we should probably do something about all this caribou. And his boat."

"I could take it all back to Chukchi in the boat if you can spare me for a few hours," Kavik said.

Active nodded. "Probably make Cowboy happy if we don't throw a bunch of bloody meat into his new plane."

"You know, Noyakuk didn't fall getting out of any boat," Kavik said as he lashed a load of caribou onto the back of Noyakuk's Yamaha.

"No? What are you thinking?"

"I used to ride a motorcycle and I took a few spills until I wised up. I know road rash when I see it, and that's an asphalt burn on his arm."

"Hm. Why lie about that?"

Kavik shrugged. "And we never told him Jesse's death was a suicide."

"I noticed that. He either assumed it or—"

"Yeah. Or he was there."

They were both silent for a moment.

"But why would he kill his best friend?" Kavik said.

Active looked at the tundra and brush around them. "And how, if he was way out here at the time?"

CHAPTER EIGHTEEN

• *Thursday, September 1* •

HOME OF DENISE SHELDON, CHUKCHI

"I'm Superman!" the toddler in the blue parka squealed as the swing flew up. The toes of his red rubber boots pointed at the sky.

"Fly, Superman!" Paul Noyakuk shouted as he gave the swing another push. His deep laughter mixed with the peal of the child's giggles.

Active and Kavik crossed the scattered patches of browning grass to the battered swing set in Denise Sheldon's backyard. Noyakuk glanced at them and caught the swing in its backward arc.

The boy kicked his feet. "Don't stop, Unca Paw! Don't stop!"

Noyakuk lifted the boy over his head and set him on his shoulders. The boy stared at Active and Kavik with what might have been resentment for ruining his fun.

"Hey, Corey, I think your mama is making you a grilled cheese sandwich," Kavik said.

"Gwilled che-e-e-se?" The boy's eyes widened.

"Sounds good, ah?" Noyakuk said. "Let's go see." The pair took off at a gentle trot for the back door.

Active and Kavik took seats at a lopsided picnic table fashioned from scrap lumber. Noyakuk returned and straddled the bench on the opposite side. A twenty-four-hour stay at the hospital had calmed him down. His shoulders were loose, his eyes a little drowsy.

"You feeling better?" Kavik asked.

Noyakuk nodded. "Back on my meds." He smiled weakly. "What happened at Ivisuk, I—Hey, Danny, thanks for bringing my meats and boat back. I filled up my mom's freezer and Denise's freezer, but I still got lots if you want some. You, too, Chief."

Kavik looked at Active, then back to Noyakuk. "Police officers can't—"

"Oh, yeah," Noyakuk cut in. "Conflict of interest, I guess." He rocked from side to side. The table flexed like it was about to collapse. He grinned and Active was reminded of the clowning figure in the photo from Jesse Apok's refrigerator.

"Jesse built this sorry piece of shit." Noyakuk ran his hand along the edge of the table, then looked toward the sky. "You wanna talk about him, ah?"

Active nodded and pulled out his notebook and pen.

"There's talk around town, maybe it's not a suicide."

"We haven't ruled anything out," Active said. "We're hoping you could help us fill in a few blanks."

"I could try," Noyakuk said, "but I wasn't here."

"Yeah, your mom said she dropped you off at the lagoon that morning early."

"Right."

Active waited for Noyakuk to volunteer more information. None came. "When was the last time you talked to Jesse?"

"Monday a week ago, before he went to work." He frowned in thought for a moment. "I never tell you that up at Ivisuk?" He stretched a hand across the top of the table, found a protruding nail head and picked at it with his thumb.

"So what time was that?" Active asked.

"Must have been around six, like I said, right before he went to work that night."

"Did he tell you if he talked to anyone else that day?"

"Nah. He was late so we didn't talk much."

"Do you know if he was expecting someone to come over the next morning?"

"Nah. But if someone was there, they would have stopped him, ah?"

Active again waited for Noyakuk to grow uncomfortable with the silence and pick up the story. Again, it didn't work. He just stared up at the sky.

"From killing himself?" Active suggested.

Noyakuk brought his eyes level with Active. "Yeah."

"Who else would come by his place besides you?"

"Just Denise whenever she bring Corey over." He shrugged. "Jesse kind of kept to himself."

"He didn't have a girl?"

"He kinda like that Evie girl, the one got killed. But he think maybe she's too good for him. She liked them *naluaqmiut*."

"What do you think of that?"

"Shit, man, women do what they do. Sometimes the grass looks greener." He shrugged again but quicker this time, more like a flinch. "I got no issues with that."

"You get along all right with those *naluaqmiut* in the Air Force?"

"The enlisted guys were okay. Sometimes they ask me about

igloos and polar bears." He grinned wide and shook his head. "We joke around, you know, they call me Eskimo Joe sometimes, but when the computers don't work, they don't want nobody else, even if it's not my job."

"How about the white officers? The ones who made the life-and-death decisions?"

Noyakuk brought his fist down on the table so hard Active's notebook bounced. "I don't want to talk about that."

"Sometimes it helps to talk it out, you know, with the nightmares—"

"How do you know—that's got nothing to do with Jesse being shot. I thought that's what you came here to talk about."

Active nodded, flipped through his notes, scribbled "nightmares," underlined it, tapped his pen against his chin.

Noyakuk shifted on his bench and the table rocked again. Finally he stood up and paced in a tight circle. "I heard you arrested that *taaqsipak* girl from the weather station. You think she had something to do with what happened to Jesse?"

There it was again, the gossip river. There was no way, ever, to stop its flow or change its direction. And now, Paul Noyakuk had tapped into it. More reason to regret he'd been too deep into "I am the caribou" to be questioned on the way back from Ivisuk.

"Like I said, we haven't ruled anything out. If it's a suicide, we just need to make sure. You said Jesse had been upset lately about not seeing his son?"

"Yeah. He had this idea Denise wasn't going to let him see Corey no more."

Active tapped his pen on the table, turned to Kavik and nodded toward the house. "Danny, let's not forget to ask her about that when—"

"Wait," Noyakuk cut in, "I didn't say Jesse knew what he was talking about. Denise didn't want him around Corey when he was drinking, but she wasn't gonna cut him off completely. I tried to tell him he wasn't making no sense, but he wouldn't listen. He was mental about it."

"Yeah?" Active asked. "Mental enough to commit suicide?"

"Yeah, I guess. Somebody killing Jesse, that doesn't make no sense. Jesse never did nothing to nobody but himself." Noyakuk looked toward the house. "He was messed up in a lot of ways, but he loved that kid. That's why I gotta try to, you know, fill that void for him." Noyakuk waved at the swing set.

"With Jesse gone, maybe you could have a family, a kid, a woman?"

Noyakuk sat down and leaned toward Active. "That's not what I meant. Corey and I are tight. I'll always be his Unca Paw. Denise doesn't know how to tell him about Jesse. She thinks I should be the one to do that. But Denise? She never want anyone but Jesse. And Jesse never want anyone but her. They just drive each other crazy, is all."

"We think Denise was the last person he talked to before—"

"Yeah, she told me he called her." Noyakuk sat up straight, folded his hands on the table. "She said he was drinking, saying crazy shit."

Active looked from Kavik to Noyakuk. "Yeah, that's what she told us too."

Noyakuk exhaled and slowly shook his head. "No one could talk sense into him when he's like that, not even Denise. She blame herself. I told her there's nothing she could have done."

"Just like there was nothing you could have done, ah?" Kavik said.

"Yeah, I was fifty miles up the Katonak when he—"

Noyakuk stared at Kavik for a couple of seconds. "But that doesn't make it any easier. I miss him so much, man." A heavy tear spilled down his cheek.

"Unca Paw!" the toddler's voice sang out from the back door. "Let's play Power Rangers!"

Noyakuk swiped the tear away with the back of his hand and stood up. "Be right there, buddy!"

"You gonna tell him about his dad?" Kavik asked.

Noyakuk took a deep breath. "Maybe I'll take him fishing, tell him then."

Kavik nodded. "That's hard, man."

Noyakuk hung his head, kicked at a pale clump of withered grass.

"Unca Paw!" the boy's voice was higher, more insistent.

Noyakuk smiled. "Gotta go."

"Thanks, Paul," Active called as Noyakuk trotted to the back door, scooped up the toddler, and carried him inside.

Active sat for a moment longer at the table, looking over his notes. "That man has the weight of the world on his shoulders."

"You think he talked to Jesse about more than what he told us?"

"Absolutely. And we have to find out who else besides Denise talked to Jesse that morning."

"Why?" Kavik asked. "There were no texts or calls during that time on his phone. Just that one last text to Evie."

"But there should have been," Active said with a satisfied half grin.

Kavik frowned and scratched behind his ear. "Oh, yeah. Jesse called Denise Sheldon and Denise called him back after he hung up."

"Someone deleted those calls, either on purpose or accidentally,"

Active said. "Maybe while they were deleting other calls on that phone."

"Other calls? But if they're deleted, they're gone, right?"

"Not from the phone-company records."

"On it, Chief."

Active's cell bleated and Cowboy's agitated voice came through the Tahoe's speaker.

"She's stalking me. You've got to do something, Nathan. She—"

"Stalking you? Who?"

"Monique Rogers."

"Monique? She didn't leave town?"

"No. And she won't leave me the hell alone. Wherever I go, there she is. I'm in the breakroom at Lienhofer, she's outside the door. I'm in the E-Z Market, she's rolling a cart down the next aisle. I'm in the drive-through at Lava Java, she pulls up behind me."

"Come on, it's Chukchi. Everybody's always in each other's business. Zero degrees of separation."

"You don't believe me?"

"Okay, where are you now?"

"At the NAPA store getting a fan belt for my truck."

"And I suppose she's staring at you over the motor oil?"

"No, she's sitting in her Jeep in the parking lot. I'm looking out the window at her right now."

"Maybe she's waiting for someone."

"I'm telling you, man, she's stalking me. If she's still out there when I'm done, I'm gonna—"

"Hold on, Cowboy. Don't go threatening anybody. We'll take care of it. Danny will"—he looked at Kavik, who was already nodding—"Danny will go talk to her right now."

CHAPTER NINETEEN

• *Friday, September 2* •

HOME OF NELDA QIVITS, CHUKCHI

Active and Grace walked through the *kunnichuk* of Nelda Qivits's cabin next to the Chukchi hospital and Grace knocked at the inner door. They stepped back a little to wait.

Being in Nelda's *kunnichuk* took Active back to his last visit with the tribal healer a few years earlier.

He was having the bullet dream, night after night. A shadowed figure would come at him with a butcher knife. He'd try to shoot, but his gun wouldn't fire. It would jerk uselessly in his hand until he woke up panting, and he would be done with sleep for that night.

The thing was, Nelda had rarely asked a question about the bullet dream or offered advice. She had never reacted to anything he said about the dream, but still her magic had worked. She would chatter away like any old *aana*, swapping idle gossip till he found himself pouring out what was on his mind. Afterward, he would feel better and the dream wouldn't come for a while. He had never figured out what the dream was about, but eventually it didn't come at all, and somehow that was because of Nelda.

They heard footsteps behind the door, then fingers at the latch, and the door creaked open. Nelda's thick cataract glasses flashed at them like headlights as she leaned her thin old frame on a thick spruce walking stick. "You come," she said, and motioned them in with an impatient wave that seemed to say they were the ones who had kept her waiting.

The cabin was hot inside, as was customary among the Inupiat, particularly if the Inupiaq in question was old. They followed as she hobbled into the tiny kitchen, the hem of her green *atiqluk* swinging. Nelda was past eighty now, Active guessed. Her short white hair was wispier and her back a little more bowed than he remembered. Kay-Chuck's Gospel Hour blared from a clock radio on the counter. Its time display blinked "12:00" in red numerals.

"I'm making sour-dock tea," Nelda announced as they took seats at her kitchen table. On the stove, water in a battered saucepan burbled as she threw in a handful of the root reputed among the *aanas* to cure almost everything.

"Too much worry, Gracie. I see it in your face." The old woman turned off Gospel Hour in the middle of "Will the Circle Be Unbroken?" and pulled three mugs from a doorless cabinet. "So, good thing you come. A winter baby is something to look forward to, like when them little *uqpiks* come up through the snow."

"It's not the baby that worries me." Grace shot Active a sideways glance. "It's Nita."

"And the ghost of your father."

"You know?" Grace asked.

"You tell me a little, Nathan tell me a little. There's talk and stories on Kay-Chuck radio from that time. Some things I put together."

Grace sat with her head bowed in silence. The pot on the stove bubbled and hissed. Grace's hair hid her face so that Active couldn't see her eyes. But her shoulders shook a little. He put his hand on hers.

Nelda poured tea, set the mugs on the table, and settled into a chair.

Active sipped the tea and for a moment the bitter taste put him back in his bullet-dream days. He took another sip and was in the present again.

Nelda slid a cup toward Grace. "I never think you're bad. You come back here, you save Nita from that man, you adopt her."

Grace raised her head and wrapped her palms around the steaming mug. "But I never told her who her mother is."

"Or her father."

"Of course not."

"Hm." The old woman leaned on her cane and rocked gently back and forth.

"She was just a little girl," Grace said. "She couldn't have handled anything like that."

"Ah, things are simple to little children, they see fish in a clear stream, no muddle-up water from adult messes."

Grace sipped at the bitter tea.

"But she's not a child anymore," Grace said. "She's thirteen, going on twenty sometimes. She hears things at school and she's asking questions."

"And you wish she never do that." Nelda nodded to herself.

"I don't have answers." She looked down at her belly, which still didn't show except when she was naked, and then only a little. "And

I don't think I can face these questions again with another child someday. Maybe I shouldn't have it."

Nelda drank her tea and set the cup down. "I think you have answers like Nita want, ah?"

Grace looked exasperated, presumably because Nelda seemed determined to ignore the main question on her mind.

Active put his hand on her shoulder and squeezed a little.

Grace sighed in apparent resignation. "But how much should she know? All of it? I mean, the pain it will cause her. And when do we tell her? And how?"

"She knows some already, ah?"

"I've . . ." Grace's fingers tightened around Active's. "We've told her that the person she thinks was her Aunt Ida shot and killed the man she thinks was her Uncle Jason. But we haven't told her why."

Nelda sipped tea, shut her eyes, rocked on the cane again. Her chin fell to her chest. Active thought she might have dozed off.

Then she spoke, her eyes still closed. "A baby starts inside, so tiny, it needs its mother's protection, but one day it just come out." She smiled. Grace strained forward. "If it know what's out here, maybe it'll stay in there, ah? But nothing can hold it back when that time come around."

Active didn't know if Nelda had switched to the pregnancy or if she was speaking in metaphors about everything else. But Grace seemed to catch on right away.

"You're right, she'll want the whole story at some point, or at least she'll think she does." Grace looked at Active. "So when she asks, we decide how much she can understand at that moment, and then we answer? We take our cue from her instead of torturing ourselves about it?"

Nelda didn't speak, but a smile creased the weathered brown skin at the corners of her dark eyes. She labored to her feet and set her empty mug in the sink. "Finished?"

"Uh, not yet." Grace looked at Active's half-full cup, took a sip from her own, and grimaced at the taste.

"I still don't know what to do about—" She looked at her stomach again, and this time she patted it.

"A little at a time is best way," Nelda said with a soft smile. "Until it's all done."

She leaned on her cane again and looked as if she couldn't decide whether to sit or stand. After a moment, she took something from a basket on the sinkboard and twisted it in a cloth.

"This sour-dock root, ah? You take it with you, keep you calm, keep the baby safe." The old lady fixed her eyes on Grace.

Grace broke her gaze, but closed her fingers around the little bundle. "Thank you, Nelda."

"Always two people make a baby." Nelda let the words hang in the steamy air. "Better if two people carry it, ah?"

"I think I'm pretty much the one—"

"Nathan knows what I mean."

Grace put her hand over his, which shook a little as he held the cup. "Nathan?"

What was this rush of emotion—anger? pain?—welling up inside him? The sour-dock tea was pulling up something as bitter as the root itself.

"You say you're ready to have the baby," he said in a near shout. "We told Nita, we told Martha. Then you say you don't know. Then you say you think you can't go through with it. I feel like a fish flopping on a line."

"I'm sorry, baby. I'm trying, but it's so hard."

Active lifted Grace from her chair and pulled her onto his lap. As he cradled her head against his shoulder, he heard Nelda walk out of the kitchen, her stick tapping the floor. A draft blew in as she opened the front door.

"You two always stay inside too much," she called. "Good afternoon for a walk, talk a little maybe."

Active tightened his arm around Grace's shoulders and pulled her close in unspoken apology for the outburst at Nelda's as they sat on a blanket draped over the hood of the Tahoe. They gazed in silence out over Chukchi and the bay beyond from their perch on Cemetery Hill, east of town on the back side of the lagoon. Then she put her arm through his and squeezed, which he took to mean, "Apology accepted."

"Much better than a walk, ah?"

"Maybe," she said. "I haven't been out here in a long time, not since Jeanie's birthday last year."

Active chided himself. Grace's older sister, along with their parents, were buried in the cemetery behind them. Jeanie had been one of Jason Palmer's victims, too. Her suicide had set off Grace's perilous journey from Chukchi to near self-destruction on Four Street to the beautiful fox-eyed survivor now at his side. He kissed her temple.

"Sorry, I didn't think. And I'm sorry for losing it back there. Like I said before, it's your call. I don't want to add to the pressure."

She squeezed his arm again. "Thank you for understanding."

The midafternoon sun glinted off the distant bay where water and sky got lost in each other. Below them, a pickup crawled across the bridge over the lagoon and up the road that looped south behind them along the bluff.

Grace snuggled her cheek into Active's neck. He lifted her chin for a kiss.

"You taste nice," she said.

He found himself stirring. "That's just the appetizer."

"There's a main course?"

He slid his hand under her blouse, across the soft swell of belly and the warm curve of breast, up to the firm berry of her nipple. "Or dessert."

"In broad daylight? I don't know."

"It's no honeymoon suite, but this thing does have a pretty big back seat." Out of the corner of his eye, Active saw the pickup, an old blue Ford, approaching along the Loop Road.

"Huh," she said. She turned and contemplated the space behind them.

The blue Ford backfired twice from out on the road. They both jumped. It drew closer and they heard country music—something about friends in low places—blaring from an open window as the truck turned onto the little side road to the cemetery. They separated and returned waves from the truck's driver and his two passengers as they went past. The truck parked thirty yards or so down the bluff.

"So . . . ?" Active said as they sat side by side, decorous now except where their thighs touched.

"Too much company, maybe?" She nodded in the direction of the pickup.

Active felt himself wilt and sighed in resignation. Grace slid her arm under his bicep and pressed her cheek to his shoulder in what he took to be sympathy, or perhaps apology.

"When's the last time you were out here?" she asked.

He thought about it for a moment. "Last spring, I think. It was when Ernie Miller got into a knockdown-drag-out with his neighbor. When he heard we were on our way, he stole the neighbor's truck and made a run for it."

"Seriously?"

Active nodded. "A true criminal mastermind. He ran out of gas right there on the Lagoon Bridge, at which point he threw in the towel and waited for us."

"Well, that's pure Chukchi." She smiled and gazed out over the wind-ruffled blue of the lagoon and the shining gray sea beyond.

"You know what sticks in my mind about that case? The truck had a busted headlight, and I couldn't stop thinking about that song they play on Kay-Chuck. 'One-Eyed Ford'?"

"Don't remind me. If I hear it one more time—"

"Seriously."

They sat in silence again. The blue Ford cranked up, turned around, and pulled past them on its way out of the cemetery. The occupants waved again and they waved back.

His fingers edged onto her thigh, then stroked the taut muscle under her jeans.

She looked at her watch. "Nita will be home from school in twenty minutes. I don't like leaving her on her own these days."

"Twenty minutes?"

"Yep."

He tilted his head toward the Tahoe's interior and raised his eyebrows. She grinned, nodded, and slid off the hood.

CHAPTER TWENTY

• *Saturday, September 3* •

FAT FRANNY'S RESTAURANT, CHUKCHI

"See what I mean?" Cowboy jabbed his finger like a dagger. "There she is. Everywhere I go." He speared a chunk of reindeer sausage with his fork and shoved it in his mouth. "Like a goddamn shadow."

A glob of melting butter flattened on the top of his pancake and slid off.

Active swiveled his head and looked across the dining room at Fat Franny's. Midday light strained through the two large windows that faced the bay and hit the BREAKFAST ALL DAY sign. The greasy smell of frying meat and eggs hung in the air. China clinked on stainless steel as a cook slammed a plate down for pickup at the kitchen window. A busboy walked by, hefting a plastic tub of dirty dishes.

At a booth in a back corner, Monique Rogers's curl cloud and dark eyes peered over a menu. She disappeared behind the menu when Active caught her eye.

"I'm going over there to ask that nut job what the fuck she

thinks she's doing." Cowboy planted his hands on the table and shoved back his chair.

Active put a hand on his arm. "No, you're not. I'll talk to her. You stay here."

"But—"

Active tightened his grip and put on his command voice. "Do. Not. Move."

Cowboy snorted and glared. But he pulled his chair back to the table.

"Ms. Rogers, I wish I could say it's a pleasure to see you." Active slid into the booth across from his recent prime murder suspect. "But I thought Officer Kavik made it clear to you that you are to stay away from Mr. Decker. What part of 'stay away' did you not understand?"

She set down the menu and took a sip of ice water. Her raspberry-colored lips curved into a smile.

"And leave this big, black cloud hanging over my reputation?" She mimed a cloud above her head. "Let everybody in town think I'm a murderer? Wouldn't that be convenient for your friend Cowboy Decker?"

"And Cowboy has what to do with your reputation, exactly?"

"What does—are you serious?" She set the glass down so hard that ice slopped onto the table.

"He says you're still following him."

"Damn straight, I am. I'm going to stay on his ass like white on rice."

"And that would be because . . . ?"

"Because I'm going to solve those murders, that's why."

Active heard footsteps approaching from behind. He turned, ready to order Cowboy back to his table.

Instead, he saw a scowling fifty-ish Inupiaq with black-rimmed glasses and a tattered denim jacket. The newcomer leaned over the table.

"What about my rights?" he said in a gravelly voice. "I'm a taxpayer in this town! What about my rights?"

Active stood, took stock of the speaker, and put out his hand. "Nathan Active, chief of Public Safety."

They exchanged the customary single-pump shake.

"Lincoln Emmonak."

"How can I help you, Mr. Emmonak?"

"It's my bike. I need it to get to work."

"Your bike?"

"Someone robbed it. I filed a report ten days ago and nobody ever call me. I never hear nothing."

"I understand your concern, sir. We'll keep an eye out for it, but a bicycle—"

"It's a Honda motorcycle, I just call it my bike. But I already got it back, after my sister spot it couple days later—"

"So your problem is . . ."

"It's all wrecked up. Whoever rob it, they crash it and mess up the front wheel. They're not cheap, you know. And now I gotta walk to work."

"What do you want me to do, Mr. Emmonak?"

"I want you to find the damn robber and make him pay to fix my bike."

"I'll have an officer canvass the area, talk to the neighbors and so on."

Emmonak nodded and raised his eyebrows. "You check out that kid next door play that loud music all time. That rap shit. I think maybe him or them losers he hang out with took it."

"I'll make a call right now," Active said.

Monique tapped a spoon on the table like an impatient girlfriend. Active looked at her and put up a finger, rolling his eyes when Emmonak wasn't looking. Monique gave a slight grin and put down the spoon.

He pulled out his cell, tapped a contact, and put up a finger. "This will just take a minute, Ms. Rogers."

Alan Long answered and Active directed him to look into the matter of Lincoln Emmonak's Honda.

Emmonak nodded and said, "'Bout time you guys earn your paychecks, all right."

"Maybe you could get Kay-Chuck to do a spot, ask people to call Public Safety if they have a tip," Active suggested.

Emmonak raised his eyebrows, yes, and said, "Thanks, Chief." He put out his hand and Active pumped it.

Active turned back to Monique as Emmonak returned to his table.

"Ms. Rogers, you were talking about solving murders—"

"Cowboy Decker did it, and I'm going to watch him like a hawk until he slips up."

"What?"

"You can't see what's staring you in the face because he's your buddy." She looked over Active's shoulder in the direction of Cowboy's table.

"And how did you come to this conclusion?"

"Think about it, Chief. Who knows about airplanes? Cowboy."

"Yes, he's a pilot, but so are about—"

"Who would have access to his own plane? Cowboy. Who knew Evie and Todd were going to be in that plane? Cowboy."

"Wait, wait. How do you know—"

"You're not the only one who asks questions, Chief." She threw out her chest, and Active wondered if she might actually pat herself on the back. "People at Lienhofer like to talk. Cowboy told everyone he and Todd were taking that plane to Fairbanks. And if Evie went instead of Cowboy, he would have to know, right? And who else would?"

"Ms. Rogers, this matter is under active police investigation. I have to caution you not to interfere."

"It's obvious he's the killer." Her eyes darted up and behind Active.

Cowboy's finger was in Monique's face before Active could turn. "You better watch your mouth, you loony tunes—"

Monique leapt to her feet and dove at Cowboy with hands spread like a tiger's paws. Active got between them and pushed the pilot back while Monique screeched, "Murderer!" and Cowboy barked, "Nut job!"

"Cowboy, get back to that table right now!" Active commanded. "Ms. Rogers, I'm going to escort you to the door. Or do you want me to arrest both of you for disorderly conduct?"

"But my food!" Monique protested. A young Inupiat waitress with a BLT on a plate stood frozen a few feet away.

"Can you fix that to go, please, miss?" Active called to the waitress.

"My treat," he told Monique as he took her elbow and steered her toward the door.

Monique cooperated well enough, even though she kept swiveling her head to keep Cowboy in sight. They waited at the door until the waitress brought the foil-wrapped sandwich. Monique tucked it into her shoulder bag.

Active pulled the door open for her. She smiled at him, then spun and shouted with such force that her whole body shook.

"You won't get away with this, Cowboy Decker! I'm taking you down, you hear me? Down!"

CHAPTER TWENTY-ONE

• Tuesday, September 6 •

ESTHER NOYAKUK'S HOME, CHUKCHI

Kavik studied the printout from the Chukchi phone company as Active steered the Tahoe along Second Street. "Esther Noyakuk. Why was Jesse calling her twenty minutes after she dropped Paul off?"

"Mother of his best friend," Active said. "No mother of his own, troubled young guy with a load on his mind. Maybe he needed a mom."

He pulled to a stop in front of Esther Noyakuk's beat-up little yellow frame house.

Kavik rested his finger on a column of numbers. "He hung up after seven seconds. Looks like around the time she would be starting work."

"So maybe she couldn't talk. But then she called him back a half hour later?"

"Yeah. That call lasted about four minutes. Interesting, ah?"

"Even more interesting, why didn't she mention it when we talked to her?"

"She was worried about Paul? Maybe it slipped her mind?"

"Not likely, with the way she felt about Jesse." Active switched off the Tahoe. "Let's find out."

Active removed the key from the ignition, and they climbed the slanted steps to the house.

Kavik pointed to the Visqueen covering a broken window. "I used to pass by here on my way to high school. Everything was always in good shape back then."

Active knocked on the door. "What happened?"

"Nobody around to help out while Paul was gone, I guess."

The yap of a small dog sounded from inside, then quieted to muffled whining and snuffling at the bottom of the door. Active knocked again. That produced more barking but no human sounds.

"Nobody home!" The voice came from between the Noyakuk house and the one next door.

Active stepped off the porch and walked around to the space between the two houses. A muscular man in his thirties wearing a torn sweatshirt and headphones was at work on the engine of a Yamaha four-wheeler.

"Chief Active. Have you seen Esther Noyakuk today?"

The mechanic pulled a headphone away from one ear. Active could hear rock music blasting out of it even from a couple of feet away.

The man squinted the Inupiat no. "Nobody since the ambulance come last night."

"Who needed an ambulance?"

The man shook his head. "They're already leaving when I get home. Maybe the old man."

"Esther's husband?"

"No, he passed a long time ago. Her father-in-law stays there. I don't see him much. Sometimes her boy bring him outside in a wheelchair and he just sit there. I think his mind is gone, all right."

The E-Z Market manager, Eldon Brown, was a tall, round, balding white man. He peered around a stack of Hunt's tomato sauce to greet Active and Kavik as they walked in. A girl Active didn't recognize was behind the cash register and a kid with a backward baseball cap and a Metallica T-shirt was rolling a handcart piled with Huggies down an aisle. The wheels screeched.

"Mr. Brown, we need to talk to one of your employees," Active said once the introductions were out of the way. "Esther Noyakuk. Is she here, or with her—"

"Oh, my." Brown shook his head. "Of course you wouldn't know. Esther's in the hospital. She had a stroke last night."

Active and Kavik exchanged a glance.

"Esther's in the hospital? We heard it might be her father-in-law. Any word on how she's doing?"

"I'm afraid not. We're all planning to visit her, but right now we're not sure if she can talk to visitors." The man shook his head. "She's always so reliable. We hardly know what to do around here without her."

He threw a pained look at the cashier, who smiled weakly. Then he looked back at Active.

"Why do you want to talk to Esther?"

The handcart stopped squealing. The stocker cocked an ear toward Active, as did the cashier.

"She might have some information we need."

"Information? About what?" Brown asked.

The Metallica fan moved a step closer, which caught the attention of his boss.

Brown threw a hard glance his way. "Those Huggies aren't going to shelve themselves."

The handcart wheels screeched back into action.

"Thanks for your time," Active said. "We'll have a couple of coffees to go."

"Sure thing, help yourselves at the station over there. But what's—well, if you have any other questions, just let me know?"

They got their coffees and headed for the exit.

"If you talk to Esther, tell her we miss her," the manager called after them.

Active eased into his seat in the Tahoe, set his coffee in the cup holder and pulled out his notebook.

"All right, take me through those phone records again, starting with Jesse's first call to Esther."

"That was at 6:56." Kavik straightened the pages on his lap and traced the lines of information with his finger. "About a half hour after she dropped Paul off at his boat, meaning she's probably at work at E-Z Mart by then. The call lasts seven seconds."

"No answer, presumably. Maybe he leaves a short voicemail?"

Kavik nodded. "Then, at 7:04, Jesse calls Denise and they talk for six minutes."

"Denise confirmed that," Active said. "According to her, he called just as she was getting home from her night shift at the Arctic Inn. He begged to see Corey and she drove over to the Pamiuktuk. She said she got there about fifteen minutes after she talked to him, so that would be around 7:30. Go on."

"At 7:32, Esther calls Jesse."

"Returning his 6:56 call, most likely," Active said.

"Most likely," Kavik said. "And they talk for almost five minutes."

"So it's a substantial conversation, not just 'Hey, I called to say hi.' Jesse's gotta still be distraught about wanting to see his son, about doing something bad like he told Denise."

"Yep," Kavik said. "And meantime, Denise is sitting out front in her Jeep with Corey. She said she waited about twenty minutes, then she called Jesse." He found the spot in the printout. "That was at 7:48 and the call lasted eleven minutes, which gets us up to 7:59."

"She said either he hung up or the call dropped. She called him back one more time and got his voice mail."

"Right," Kavik said. "Three minutes later, at 8:02."

Active looked at his notes again. "And an hour after that Jesse's dead. The upstairs neighbor heard the gunshot at nine. So, 7:59 is the last time Jesse talked to anyone but the killer. And Denise said she didn't hear anybody else there, just the TV."

"And Paul said he didn't know of anyone who would come over to see him."

"Maybe Jesse mentioned someone to Esther."

Active's cell pinged and a text from Grace came up. GOT CALL FROM NITA'S TEACHER. FALLING ASLEEP IN CLASS. TIME TO TAKE PHONE AWAY AGAIN? REMIND HER IT'S IN MY NAME? A PRIVILEGE? TALK WHEN YOU GET HOME?

K, he texted back, reflecting that it had become almost unconscious now, dealing with family stuff no matter what else was going on.

"I sure hate to bother Esther in the hospital," Kavik said. "But I guess we gotta?"

Active was silent, studying the list of calls in his notebook.

"Chief?" Kavik said.

Active put up a hand, and Kavik waited him out.

"Why didn't she tell us about any of this?" he said finally.

Kavik chewed his lip for a moment, then frowned. "Good question, actually."

"What if it wasn't Esther?" Active said.

Kavik frowned. "Ah?"

"Give me that printout." Active put his phone on speaker and punched in Esther's number from the phone records.

It rang four times, then a male voice came on.

"Hello? Hello? Who is it?"

Active tapped off and looked at Kavik. "Recognize that voice?"

"Paul Noyakuk!"

"Using his mother's phone."

"Which means if it was him calling Jesse that morning, he was not fifty miles up the river."

"Not if he had cell reception," Active said. "So, yeah, we definitely gotta—"

"Talk to Esther?"

"Let's go." Active started the Tahoe and was about to pull away when his cell came to life again.

"Yeah, Lucy? What? *Arii*, that woman. Tell her I'm on my way." He tapped off the call and looked at Kavik with a grimace.

"What?"

"Monique Rogers is apparently at Public Safety, raising hell and claiming she's solved our case."

"Which one?"

"Not clear," Active said. "I'll drop you at the hospital and go find out while you talk to Esther."

"Better you than me, boss."

Active put the Tahoe back in gear, then shifted to neutral again. Something was tugging at the corner of his mind, a loose end. He knew the feeling, but what was he missing?

"Oh, yeah," he said. "Esther's father-in-law. Make sure the EMTs did something with him last night."

"They wouldn't just leave him alone in the house."

"So one would hope. But this is Chukchi."

CHAPTER TWENTY-TWO

• Tuesday, September 6 •

PUBLIC SAFETY DEPARTMENT, CHUKCHI

Monique Rogers dropped into an orange plastic chair and scooted up to the edge of Active's desk.

"I rushed over as soon as it popped into my head, Chief."

"Why thank you, Ms. Rogers. Would you like some coffee? Of course, it's not Arabica, but—"

"No, no, no, but thanks. It's just like you tried to tell me when you and the other officer came by the weather station. Where is that nice young officer, anyway?"

"At the hospital."

"Oh, my. He's not hurt, is he?"

Active almost smiled at the show of concern. Real or brownnosing?

"Officer Kavik's fine. He's out on a case. But tell me, what brings you in today?"

"Officer Kavik said I should play back that night in July in my mind like it was a movie, and that way maybe I'd see what I saw then."

"The night before the plane crash, when you ran past Lienhofer's?"

She nodded. Her curls bounced.

"I kept picturing Jesse on that ladder over the wing like a scene from a movie, just like Officer Kavik said. There Jesse was as I ran past, I must have been about thirty yards away. I waved like I always do."

"And he waved back?"

"No—and that's the thing. It was almost like he went out of his way not to turn in my direction."

"And that's what—"

"That's not the best part."

A gust of air rattled in as the door opened and Lincoln Emmonak burst into the room.

Lucy Brophy stood behind him, hands in the air. "Sorry, Nathan. I told him you were busy."

"It's okay, Lucy." She shut the door. "Mr. Emmonak, what's going on?"

Monique jumped out of her chair.

"You again!" she shouted. She put her palms out and air-pushed as Emmonak walked toward Active's desk. "Hold it right there, buddy."

Emmonak stopped in his tracks and stared at her, then at Active.

"You can't just come in and interrupt every time I'm having an important conversation," she said. "What are you, stalking me?"

Emmonak's eyes pleaded for help.

Active pointed to an empty chair beside his desk. "Mr. Emmonak, have a seat. And make it brief, please."

"No, he has to leave." Monique glared at Active, then at the intruder. "You have to leave right now. We're conducting a murder investigation here."

"Ms. Rogers, sit down."

Active swept his arm toward her chair. She sat.

"*I* am conducting an investigation—not you, not we, I. Me. I'm sure Mr. Emmonak will only be a couple of minutes and then you will have my complete attention."

Monique rolled her eyes and slumped in the chair. She threw one leg over the other and started pumping the foot up and down with such fury that Active thought she might lose a shoe.

Active turned to his other visitor.

"Mr. Emmonak, what can I do for you?"

"I never hear a word about that robber take my bike." He pushed his black-rimmed glasses up on the bridge of his nose and puffed out his chest. A seam of his worn denim jacket separated at the shoulder. "What are you doing about it?"

"Mr. Emmonak, it's only been three days since we talked. I know Officer Long spoke to all your neighbors. Where is your place again?"

"The Swan Apartments, number three."

"And where was your motorcycle found?"

"The other side of town. At them Pamiuktuk Apartments where my sister live, like I try tell you."

A distant bell pealed in Active's head.

"The Pamiuktuk? August twenty-third?"

"That's right. Someone sure have to get there in a hurry, all right, wreck my bike, then leave it till my sister look out her kitchen window, see it in them weeds."

Now the sound in his head was more like a fire bell.

"Mr. Emmonak, I'm going to pull your file and see if we have any description of the person who took your motorcycle."

"And wrecked it."

"Like I said, sir, I'm going to see if we have any description of the alleged thief. And I will do that as soon as I'm finished talking with Ms. Rogers. If you would please wait outside my office, I'll let you know what I find. Ask Ms. Brophy to get you some coffee, okay?"

Emmonak nodded and shuffled out with a parting glare at Monique.

Active slapped his desk. "So, Ms. Rogers. You were about to get to the best part?"

"That's right. You see, it wasn't just that Jesse didn't wave back. He didn't have the right body type. This guy was average built, average height, not tall and lean like Jesse. And he was wearing a ball cap."

"Maybe Jesse looked different because he was on the ladder?"

"No, it wasn't Jesse. It was Cowboy!"

"Cowboy? Did you see his face?"

"No, but I could tell by his body type. Oh, he was sneaky, he tried to cover up that leather bomber he always wears with a big camo jacket. But it was him, all right."

Active's eyes widened. "Camo? You sure?"

"A bulky, olive drab, camo field jacket. I got him. Your buddy Cowboy Decker is the killer. He's the one who sabotaged that plane." She squared her shoulders and raised her chin.

"Thank you, Ms. Rogers. This is some very helpful information."

Monique blinked hard. "So you're gonna arrest him, right?"

"Ms. Rogers, this is the first murder investigation you've been involved in, so you may not realize that there are certain things we have to do to build a case."

He waited for her to make a move toward the door. She stayed in her seat.

"So if you'll let me get to my work? I really do appreciate the information."

Monique stood. "I cracked the case, didn't I, Chief?"

"Oh, yes, Ms. Rogers, 'cracked' is definitely the applicable word here."

He stood and she walked out, head high.

Active pulled out his notebook and was flipping through it when the door opened again. He braced himself for another round with Monique. But, no, Kavik came in and hung his rain-dampened jacket on the back of the door. "Esther Noyakuk confirmed it, Chief. Her account but Paul's phone."

"How is Mrs. Noyakuk?"

"She's expected to be discharged at the end of the week." Kavik poured himself a cup of coffee. "I saw Monique Rogers on her way out. More nonsense about Cowboy being our killer, I'm guessing?"

"Actually, we may have a blind squirrel on our hands."

Kavik's look said he didn't get it.

"You know. Even a blind squirrel finds a nut once in a while? You've never heard that?"

Kavik squinted the *no*. "Probably a white thing, *naluaqmiiyaaq*. But I get it. So she's abandoned her stalking career?"

"Stalking!" Active jumped up from behind his desk. "I forgot all about Lincoln Emmonak."

"He's gone. He was giving Lucy a hard time, something about his rights. He finally said he didn't have to time to wait around for a do-nothin' cop, and then he up and left. What's his deal?"

"Another disgruntled citizen demanding instant justice." Active pulled a folder from a cabinet and opened the slender file.

"Somebody stole his motorcycle and wrecked it and he wants us to find the culprit."

"I guess we can get back to that after we close out the murder invest—"

"No, we're going to look into it now." Active thumbed through a couple of pages in the file on his desk and scanned the type.

"A stolen motorcycle? Why?"

"Because of the date it was taken, August twenty-third. Where it was taken from, the Swan Apartments. Where it was found, the Pamiuktuk Apartments. And"—Active lifted a page from the file—"here it is. Alan's interview with one of Emmonak's neighbors, Perry Starkman, a.k.a. Salt-T P."

"Ah, Chukchi's own rapper wannabe."

"You know this guy?"

"I caught his act at the community center. I gotta admit, the kid can bust a rhyme."

Active stared at Kavik and tried to picture him at a rap show.

"So what did he tell Long?" Kavik went on.

Active read from the statement. "I see that guy took the old man's scooter. It was seven o'clock. Got to be at work seven-thirty. I opened the window to have a smoke. My brother don't allow no smoking in the place. That old Emmonak guy, he's a pain in the ass, always bitching my music's too loud. So when I see someone take his wheels, I think it's funny. Like what they call karma, all right."

"Good notes. Did Mr. P describe the thief?"

"Yeah." Active summarized from the file. "Heavy camo jacket, blue patch on the shoulder, rifle in a sling."

Kavik's jaw dropped. "So Paul was in two places at the same time?"

"The way I put it together, he's headed out in his boat and he gets a call from Jesse," Active said. "Esther has just dropped him off and is on her way to work. So as far as she knows, he's gone."

"So he can't take the call for some reason, maybe the outboard's too loud. He shuts down and calls back." Kavik paused in thought. "And Jesse tells him something that makes him decide to get to Jesse's place in a hurry. He comes back in the boat, takes his gun, starts running. He spots the motorcycle by Lincoln Emmonak's door, hops on, and he's on his way to the Pamiuktuk."

"And in such a hurry he wrecks the Honda on the way."

"Takes a fall, scrapes his wrist on the asphalt," Kavik said.

"Somewhere close by the Pamiuktuk, maybe he hits that big pothole that one witness mentioned. Who was—"

"Lester Anderson, the gallbladder guy."

"That's him, the one who was in surgery," Active said. "Anyway, the Honda's busted up, but Paul doesn't want to leave it in the street. Says here in the file it's a 125. That's not a very big motorcycle, right?"

"Closer to a moped, actually."

"So it's light enough that he can muscle it up to the building," Active said. "I spotted it out the back door in some weeds when we were at the crime scene. It didn't click until now."

"So he had time to kill Jesse, set it up to look like suicide, get back to his boat, and head up to Ivisuk. No one knows about his side trip."

"In two places at once."

"But why would Paul Noyakuk kill his best friend?"

"Monique Rogers may have helped us with that, although not on purpose. She came in today to tell me she had a clearer memory of what she saw that night when Cowboy's plane was being fueled up before Evie and Todd took off for Fairbanks."

"And?"

"She remembered that the guy fueling the plane didn't look like Jesse. He was average height, not tall like Jesse, and he wasn't as skinny. And he was wearing a big camo jacket."

"So when Jesse said he was at work that night—"

"He told us he saw Cowboy because he assumed Cowboy would be there and he told us he saw Pete Boskofsky because normally Pete wouldn't be out of town. Jesse couldn't have known neither of them were at Lienhofer's because he wasn't there himself. Somehow Noyakuk was filling in for him."

"But how do we know Monique isn't just making this up to get herself off the hook?"

"Because we never told her about the camo jacket. She doesn't know who wears it. She convinced herself it was Cowboy in disguise."

"But Paul Noyakuk—why would he want to bring down that plane? He wouldn't have known Evie would be flying it instead of Cowboy. And as far as we know, there's no connection between him and Todd Brenner."

"Let's bring him in and find out. We'll check Lienhofer's first."

They were pulling into the parking lot at Lienhofer Aviation when Active's cell bleated. He took the call.

"We're taking a detour," he told Kavik. "There's a fight at the Arctic Dragon—Lincoln Emmonak and Perry Starkman."

"You mean Salt-T P?"

"The one and only."

CHAPTER TWENTY-THREE

· *6:00 P.M., Tuesday, September 6* ·

ARCTIC DRAGON RESTAURANT, CHUKCHI

A short, wiry, twenty-something Inupiaq in a white undershirt and baggy pants was slamming Lincoln Emmonak onto a table when Active and Kavik waded into the melee at the Arctic Dragon. A canister of sugar lay on the floor with its contents fanned out across the linoleum. Emmonak cursed and kicked, but gained no traction as his feet slipped on the white grit.

An Asian teenager in a waitress outfit pressed her back against the red- and gold-flecked wallpaper. Kyung Kim, an elderly Korean man with a stained apron and a liver-spotted bald head, sidestepped back and forth in the center of the restaurant, waving his arms and shouting. "You stop now! You make mess! You bust up my place!"

Active motioned him away from the action.

A half-dozen men ringed the table, egging on the combatants and knocking over water glasses and bowls of soy-sauce packets. A couple of chairs were overturned, and the shards of a broken dish were scattered across the floor between the tables. When the spectators spotted the uniforms and badges, they backed off and shut up.

"Perry Starkman! Get off him!" Active seized Salt-T P by the collar and yanked him backward.

Kavik helped the older man to a chair. "You all right, Mr. Emmonak?"

"*Arii*, you shouldn't have stopped me," Emmonak growled. "I was gonna beat his skinny ass."

"You gonna beat my ass, old man?" Starkman lunged forward.

Active yanked him back. The blue bandanna tied around his head had slipped down over one eye, making him look more comical than otherwise. Active pushed him into a chair. Kavik eased up from behind and cuffed one of his wrists to the chair with what struck Active as admirable deftness.

"You and your low-life friends, too." Emmonak motioned at the subdued cheering section, then lapsed into a coughing fit.

"I need a cigarette," he wheezed.

"You can't smoke in a public facility in Chukchi, and nobody's beating anybody's ass," Active said. "Now, Mr. Starkman, what happened here?"

"It's Salt-T P."

"What happened, Mr. P?"

"He pulled a knife on me." Starkman made another lunge.

Kavik jerked him back into the chair.

"Wasn't no knife, was a screwdriver," Emmonak said. "Don't need no knife for this little piece of *anaq*."

Another lunge from Starkman, another yank by Kavik, this time with enough force to bounce Salt-T P's head off the back of the chair.

"Where's the screwdriver?" Active asked.

The waitress pointed under one of the tables.

"What's your name, miss?"

"Amy Lee." She spoke softly with lowered eyes.

"Did you see what happened?"

She nodded. "Lots of shouting, these two." She pointed at Starkman and Emmonak. "Then they push each other back and forth,
back and forth."

Amy mimed it out for them.

"Mr. Kim, he call 9-1-1. Then this one"—she nodded at Starkman—"he point at another man was in here and they yell at each
other and then that other man run out. That's when that one
there"—she pointed at Emmonak—"pull out the screwdriver. The
other one knock it out of his hand and push him on the table."

Kavik picked up the screwdriver and dropped it into a baggie.

"That your screwdriver, Mr. Emmonak?" Active asked.

Emmonak nodded.

"You try to hurt Mr. Starkman with it?"

"*Arii,* that piece of *anaq* had it coming. Damn thief!"

"I didn't take your fucking scooter!"

"Motorcycle!" Emmonak thundered. "I ask him what he tell that
officer question all my neighbors. He don't want to tell me. I think
he's the one take my bike!"

"I told him I never!"

"Yeah, he say somebody else take it," Emmonak said. "That
other guy sitting over by the door."

Active glanced at the empty tables around the door. "What guy?"

"These jackasses scare him away." Emmonak waved at the gag-
gle of fight fans.

"Native guy?"

"Yeah. That Esther Noyakuk's boy. This one." Emmonak jabbed his finger at Starkman. "I think he's the one take it. This Stinky P here."

"Salt-T P," Starkman spat back.

"You mean Paul? Paul Noyakuk was here?" Active asked.

Emmonak nodded. "Yeah, that's him."

"Mr. Starkman, you recognized Paul Noyakuk?"

"Yeah. He's that guy I seen taking the bike. Got on that same camo jacket with the star on the sleeve."

"Mr. Starkman, you know Paul Noyakuk?"

"Kinda, yeah." He shrugged. "This is Chukchi, ah?"

"When Officer Long questioned you about the motorcycle theft, you described the man who took it. Why didn't you say it was Paul Noyakuk?"

"He never ask what his name was. Anyway, what I want to get him in trouble over some old man's scooter?"

"Motorcycle!" Emmonak hissed.

"I know a fuckin' scooter when I see one," Starkman said.

Kavik put his hand on Emmonak's shoulder to head off any renewal of hostilities.

Active turned to the waitress. "You said Mr. Starkman here was arguing with Paul Noyakuk, the guy by the door. What did Mr. Noyakuk say?"

"He say, 'You make mistake. You were drunk or something.' Then he run out. He come in here sometimes. Nice guy, gets fried rice for his mom."

Active threw Kavik a satisfied look. "Danny, let's wrap this up. We've got to get over to the hospital. You guys"—he pointed at the spectators—"you probably got this whole thing going in the first place. Get out of here, and don't be starting trouble somewhere else. You do, you'll all end up together in one of my cells and you can fight each other for the top bunk."

The men threw him sullen looks and headed for the door.

"What about me?" Starkman stood halfway up, still cuffed to the chair.

"You stay where you are."

Starkman plopped down again.

"Are you two pressing assault charges against each other?"

Emmonak stamped his foot and looked ready to spit. "*Arii*, I could let it go this time, all right. But he stole my bike and wrecked it all up and now he gotta pay for it."

"Mr. Emmonak, he didn't steal your motorcycle. Now, Mr. Starkman, Mr. Emmonak here is willing to forgive and forget. How about you?"

"But this was assault with a deadly weap—"

"Mr. Starkman."

Another shrug. "Nah, I ain't pressing no charges."

"Danny, call Alan to take Mr. Emmonak home. I want as much space as possible between him and Mr. Starkman before I let him go."

"You mean I gotta stay chained up like this?" Starkman protested.

"Danny can uncuff you, but you stand by the door and don't go out until Mr. Emmonak is out of sight."

Kavik uncuffed Starkman. He rubbed his wrist and flexed his fingers.

Kim rushed up to Active. "What about my place? Who gonna pay for all this?"

Active surveyed the destruction.

"Mr. Kim, you give me an estimate of the damages and Mr. Starkman and Mr. Emmonak will split the bill." He said it loud enough that there could be no lack of clarity for the two trouble-makers. "If they don't pay up within two weeks, you let me know and I'll arrest them."

He glared at the two combatants. "You hear me?"

"*Arii,*" Emmonak began. "But I—"

"I said I'll arrest you."

Emmonak shut his mouth and both men raised their eyebrows in the Inupiat yes. Emmonak marched out.

As Active and Kavik left the restaurant, Alan Long pulled in and parked next to the Tahoe.

"Hey, look," Kavik said.

A white carton lay a few inches from Long's front bumper. Fried rice and garlic chicken spilled out across the gravel.

Kavik squatted for a closer look. "Looks like somebody ditched his takeout." He touched the carton. "Still warm."

"Noyakuk knows his story is falling apart," Active said. "We have to find him."

Kavik nudged the spilled takeout with his toe. "Probably won't be at the hospital."

"Nope."

Long jumped out of his Tahoe and escorted a sour-faced Lincoln Emmonak to the passenger door.

"But just in case," Active told Kavik, "have Alan take you to the hospital before he takes Mr. Emmonak home. If Paul's not there, maybe his mother will know where he is. I'll check his boat."

Active pulled up to the spot at the north end of the seawall where Esther Noyakuk had described dropping her son off on the beach for his hunting trip to Ivisuk.

Half a dozen boats were tied up along the shore, including the aluminum drop front with the red Evinrude that he and Kavik had loaded with Noyakuk's gear and four-wheeler and caribou meat at Ivisuk.

He pulled his rig into the parking lot of an apartment building across from the bay and waited.

Twenty minutes passed with no sign of Noyakuk. Kavik called to say Noyakuk hadn't come by the hospital, either.

"Check Esther's house," Active told Kavik. "If he's going back to Ivisuk, he may want to pick up some gear. Take Long with you. If Noyakuk's there, call me immediately."

Active's phone sounded again a few minutes later and Grace's picture came up.

"Nathan," she said. "Nita's gone."

"Gone? Maybe she just took Lucky for a walk."

"No." Active could hear her rapid breathing. "I was late getting off work. I called home and asked her to order a pizza and we were gonna watch *The Hunger Games* again. That's when she told me."

"Told you what?"

Grace's voice broke. "That little bi—that little Mindy put something about me shooting Jason on Facebook, and now it's all over the school, and Nita's—well, you can imagine how she's feeling. I tried to calm her down, I told her we'd talk about it when you and I got home, but she said she didn't want to talk, that she—"

She drew in a sharp breath that was half sob. "—that she, ah, doesn't want me to be her mom anymore."

"That's what kids say when they get upset. She didn't mean—"

"Then where is she? She took her backpack, her iPad, and Lucky. And she's not answering her phone."

"At least we know she left of her own accord."

"Is that supposed to make me less terrified?"

"Have you called her friends?"

"Of course." A touch of exasperation was in her voice now. "None of them saw her after school."

"None of her girlfriends. But what about—"

"Stacy! I'm going over there right now." Keys jangled in the background. "We've got to talk to her, Nathan. When are you coming home?"

A couple of seconds ticked past before he spoke. "Baby, we're kind of in the thick of it with this murder case. I may not make it back at all tonight."

"But I can't do this by myself. You have to—"

"How about you see if she's at Stacy's and ask his foster mom if she can stay overnight, assuming appropriate sleeping arrangements, of course. She'll have time to cool off, you'll have time to think this out, and we can talk to her when I do get home. Meantime, I'll call Ms. Savok and get her to make Mindy take down that Facebook post and—"

"But I can't—not—how are we—"

"We'll figure it out. Call me when you find her, okay? Or if you can't."

Two four-wheelers roared past, the only perceptible movement other than passing seagulls he had seen since beginning the stakeout.

He started the Tahoe. His phone bleated again.

This time it was Kavik. "He's not at home."

"Nothing out here, either."

"But we might have something. Esther's cousin is staying at the house to take care of the old man while Esther's in the hospital.

She showed me where Paul keeps his stuff. It doesn't look like he packed up for any kind of trip."

"And where's he going to go without his boat?"

"Exactly. But it looks like he did take one thing."

"What's that?"

"His gun."

CHAPTER TWENTY-FOUR

Denise Sheldon stood working at a keyboard behind the Arctic Inn's front counter of polished red wood. Her crimson-streaked hair was pulled back in a neat, glossy ponytail. She wore a crisp, white collared blouse with a gold nametag.

In the empty lobby, a row of cup-shaped chairs in shades of light and lighter green were arranged in an arc. A mural of spruce trees covered a wall that curved around one side of the room. Piano music tinkled softly from somewhere among broad, pale green light fixtures that seemed to float against the ceiling like giant lily pads.

Denise looked up with a professional smile. "Good even—" The smile vanished at the sight of the three officers. Nearby, an elevator dinged to a stop. A housekeeper trundled a cart out and down a hall.

Kavik and Long hung back as Active leaned on the counter. "Ms.

Sheldon, we're looking for Paul Noyakuk. When's the last time you saw him?"

"That day, was it Thursday? When you came by to talk to him? He was going to take Corey fishing on Saturday, all right, but he never show up. I never even hear from him."

"We went by your house on the way here. Nobody answered the door."

"My mom and Corey went up to Katonak yesterday to visit her sister. Why you wanna find Paul?"

"He may not be thinking clearly right now, and he could be a danger to himself or someone else."

Denise's eyes widened and her hands flew to her mouth.

"Do you have any idea where he might be? Who would he go to if he needed help?"

Denise shook her head. "I don't know . . . no one, I don't think. Except maybe Jesse?"

Tears spilled out, and she grabbed a tissue from a box beside the computer. The desk phone rang and she answered: "Arctic Inn, your home away from home in Northwest Alaska. How can I help you?"

Active stepped back from the counter and turned to his partner. "Who else does he have a connection with?"

"Nobody," Kavik said. "Always been pretty much a loner, as far as I know."

Long raised his eyebrows in agreement.

Active flipped through his notebook to the pages he had dog-eared while sitting in his rig by the bay, one dog-ear for every interview in which Paul Noyakuk's name came up.

"Delilah, nope. Jesse, nope. Not Esther, nope. Wait—Loralei!"

"The mother of the little girl that died—the one he thought was his," Kavik said.

"He didn't even mention her when we talked to him—only his mom did."

"Too much pain there?" Kavik said. "The daughter they lost. Maybe they can't even talk to each other now?"

"I'm gonna go see her," Active said. "You two stay here in case Noyakuk shows up. I didn't want to alarm Ms. Sheldon, but he's armed and she might be in danger."

"But, if he's at Loralei's—"

"If I need help, I'll call you."

Active's phone pinged. He took it out and read the text as he crossed the lobby toward the exit. NITA SAFE AT STACY'S! FOSTER MOM WILL LOOK OUT FOR HER TILL MARTHA CAN PICK HER UP IN MORNING.

He studied the screen and frowned. MARTHA? WHY? he texted back.

MADE THE APPOINTMENT, LEAVING FOR ANCHORAGE ON MORNING JET, her next text read. YOU DON'T NEED TO COME, SOMETHING I HAVE TO DO MYSELF. SORRY, BABY.

He tapped CALL in the message window. It went straight to voicemail.

He stared at the screen, wondering when she had made the appointment and why she hadn't told him till now and what she had told Nita and Martha and what else there was to say. He could think of nothing and tapped off the call.

A few minutes later, Active knocked on the door of a sky-blue cottage set a few yards back from the road, tucked between the airport and the lagoon. Clumps of aspen leaned in to the roof on both sides like frail arms trying to protect the little house.

A dog barked from across the road, then a second and third joined the chorus. After two or three minutes of knocking and yelling "Police!" and "Loralei Howell? It's Chief Active!" without result, he stepped down the sagging front steps and headed for the Tahoe.

A woman dressed in black was walking in from the road. Raven hair slashed with blue was pulled up at the back of her head with a silver comb. She wore lipstick of a blue so deep it was almost black. A tiny star was tattooed at the outer corner of her right eye, and a spider web adorned her neck.

She planted her knee-high boots on the gravel of the driveway and put her hands on the hips of her skinny jeans. Sequins in a shape of a skull sparkled from her denim jacket.

"What he done now?" she demanded.

"Loralei Howell?"

She gave an impatient nod.

"Chief Active. Can we—"

"I know who you are."

"Can we go inside and talk?"

"Why not?"

He followed the rolling hips up the steps and into the house. The interior was a single big room except for a walled-in bathroom at a back corner. Active could see a black and white striped shower curtain and a furry red rug.

A couch covered in fake blue velvet occupied the middle of the room. To one side was a double bed with a white iron frame. On the other side, a pile of stuffed animals on the floor surrounded a silver-framed photograph of a little girl with dancing black eyes and a mischievous smile set off by deep dimples. A shrine to the lost one, Active surmised.

The three front walls, painted pistachio-green, were adorned with more photos of the girl. In what looked to be the most recent, she crinkled her nose and grinned, showing the gap from a missing front tooth.

"Have a seat," Loralei called from behind an open refrigerator door in the kitchen corner. "Want a soda?" The walls there were sunflower yellow.

"No, thanks," he answered, blinking against the color overload. He sank down into a corner of the blue couch.

She returned with a tall red-and-black can of punched Rockstar, plopped down beside him, and set the can on the floor.

Active pulled out his notebook and pen. "When's the last time you saw Paul Noyakuk?"

"Why you asking about him?"

"You said, 'what's he—'"

"I meant Benton Nelson, my boyfriend. My sometime boyfriend. When he's not being an asshole. Which is always."

"Oh, Benton Nelson." Active pulled up the memory of a tall, good-looking kid with a Pittsburgh Steelers hat and a shiny slash of bare skin through his left eyebrow where someone had cut him with a knife. He had never been in major trouble, just minor fights and property damage, except for when he had set an abandoned house on fire. And, even then, the owner had thanked him for getting rid of it.

"This isn't about Benton. I'm looking for Paul Noyakuk. Have you been in touch?"

"Not since we had the memorial at Easter for our baby, our little Hershey."

Active maintained a respectful expression at the sound of the name. "I'm terribly sorry for your loss. Can I ask what happened to your daughter?"

"This last winter she come down with some kind of cold, a bad one, always coughing, sound like a seal barking. I take her to the clinic, the doctor say she doesn't need to go in the hospital, just put her in the bathroom, run the shower, let her breathe the steam. I did that couple times, but she get worse and pretty soon she almost can't breathe. I take her to the emergency room and they rush her in the back. Then after while the doctor come out and say, 'Sorry,' and that's it. She's alive when I bring her in and then she's dead."

She told the story with a deadpan face, like she was talking about a TV episode that wasn't too interesting. Maybe Esther had been right. Maybe Loralei didn't care about the girl like a normal woman would. But, then again, he had never seen grief look the same twice.

"Did Paul know she was sick?"

Loralei took a drink of Rockstar, put a hand on her chest and gave a slight burp. "No. Paul never find out till he's back from Iraq and then she's already dead. That's why we have the memorial service, because he want to say goodbye."

"How did he take it?"

Loralei set the drink down and her face became serious, eyes wide. "He was so mad at first. He's smashing stuff and throwing things, make me real scare. Then he just don't talk to no one no more."

"He was angry with you?"

"No. He was angry with that doctor. He blame the doctor for everything. He say that doctor is like those *naluaqmiut* in Iraq, blow up that school with all them little girls in it. He say that doctor don't care about little girls if they're not white. He say he wish he could blow up that doctor."

"What was his name?"

"*Arii*, what was it? That cute one. Dr. Todd."

"Todd Brenner."

"Yeah, that's him."

"Did Paul say how he would blow him up?"

"Nah, Paul was always saying crazy things after he got back. He wasn't right no more, you know? I never talk to him much since he get like that. I have a job now, cleaning offices. I gotta go on with my life."

"Do you have any idea where he might be right now? Where he's staying, maybe?"

"Nope."

She took another drink.

Back in his rig, Active punched up Kavik on his phone.

"She know where Noyakuk is?" Kavik asked.

"No idea," Active said. "But listen to this: she says he wanted to quote, unquote 'blow up' Todd Brenner because he blamed Todd for his daughter's death."

"Shit. That's motive."

"Yeah. What's the situation there?"

"Quiet until a couple of minutes ago. Some irate lady guest is giving Denise hell about something."

"Ah, the pleasures of the hospitality industry. Look, I need to swing by the house and check on Grace. Call me if something breaks, otherwise I'll be there in fifteen minutes or so."

Active steered the Tahoe slowly around a curve and the lagoon came into view. He had just pulled up in front of the house and was bracing himself for what lay ahead when his phone sounded off. It was Kavik.

"Chief, that irate guest. She was complaining about someone in the next room smoking in what's supposed to be a smoke-free hotel."

"Uh-huh?"

"Thing is, Denise says that room's supposed to be vacant. But the lady insisted, said she saw a guy in there when she knocked on the door to complain about the smoke aggravating her asthma. He cursed her out and slammed the door in her face."

"Did you get a description of this phantom smoker?"

"Yep. Native guy, goatee, camo jacket."

Active gunned his engine and spun the Tahoe in a half donut to head back to the Arctic Inn.

"I'm on the way. Stay with Denise till I get there. Find out the number and location of that vacant room and which rooms are occupied on that floor right now. Then get the manager to take those guests to the lobby. Quietly."

CHAPTER TWENTY-FIVE

• *9:45 P.M., Tuesday, September 6* •

ARCTIC INN, CHUKCHI

Active banged his forearm on the dark-red door of Room 112. Kavik stood to the side, hand on the butt of his Glock. "Paul Noyakuk, open up! It's Chief Active!"

His pulse picked up. Maroon-carpeted hallway stretched off on either side, deserted and quiet. No sound came from the other side of the door.

He banged again.

"Paul! We don't want you or anyone else to get hurt. Open the door."

The soda machine down the hall hummed and rattled. A light flickered overhead.

Still nothing from the room. Not the scuff of a shoe, not a grunt or a mutter.

He had sent Long outside to watch the window of Room 112 from behind his department Tahoe.

Active pulled a key card out of his pocket and slipped it into the lock. The tiny light turned green and the lock clicked. He flipped the handle and pushed. The door opened a couple of inches and banged against the security bar.

He stepped back and shouted through the crevice. "Paul, open the door. We need to talk."

Nothing.

He pulled the door toward him till it was just shy of latching. Then he stepped back and nodded at Kavik.

Kavik cocked his leg, and slammed his heel into the door. There was a slight crack, but the security bar held.

On his third kick, it didn't. The door banged open.

Active drew his Glock and peered in. He could see the green and burgundy pattern of the cover on a corner of the bed. The smell of cigarette smoke lingered in the air. The hair rose on the back of his neck. Was Noyakuk hiding somewhere, rifle trained on the doorway?

He took a step inside, Kavik a step behind, both of their guns drawn. The bathroom was to their right, its door open to the inside, flush against the wall. The shower curtain was pulled back, the bath mat neatly hung over the rim of the tub. No one hiding there.

Active moved along the right wall. Kavik moved to his left where the mirrored doors of a closet reflected the rest of the room. It was empty.

Active trained his pistol on the closet and Kavik slid the doors back one at a time. The closet was empty, except for an ironing board and a row of wooden hangers.

Suddenly, he caught a flicker of motion in the corner of his eye and spun around, Glock pointed, finger on the trigger. But it was only the room's gray, insulated drapes billowing in at the window.

Active holstered his gun and drew them back. He leaned out into the cooling air of the dying twilight.

"Clear!" he called. "He's gone."

Long emerged from behind the Tahoe and walked toward the hotel.

Denise Sheldon sat on one of the light green chairs in the lobby, wringing her hands and sniffling back tears. Active faced her with his notebook balanced on one knee.

Kavik and Long were questioning housekeepers and bell boys in offices behind the front desk. The guests who'd been cleared from the rooms near 112 waited in a little conference room off the lobby.

"Ms. Sheldon," Active said. "We need to find out how Paul Noyakuk got into that room. If you helped him in any way, you need to tell me now."

Denise shook her head and gasped out her answer between sobs. "Paul? I don't know anything about that. I just came on shift at eight o'clock right before you walked in."

"We can check that. If you're lying, you'll be in serious trouble."

"*Arii*, what he do?" she wailed.

"It's possible he had something to do with Jesse's death—"

"Paul? But he couldn't have. They were best friends."

Before Active could continue, a woman in a housekeeper's uniform ran from the office area, across the lobby, and out the front door. Kavik followed and stopped at Active's chair.

"We know how Noyakuk got in. That housekeeper that just ran out left the window open when she cleaned that room around three this afternoon. She snuck a smoke on duty and forgot to close it when she left."

The manager, a middle-aged Inupiaq with a thin mustache and a lavender shirt, came up. "Chief, how much longer before we can let our guests back into their rooms and get our people back to work?"

"A few more minutes," Active said.

Denise turned to the manager. "I don't think I can work tonight, Mr. Timmons," she sobbed.

"Denise, I need you here," the manager said. "Otherwise I'm the one who has to—"

"I—I can't do it, Mr. Timmons."

A phone rang at the front desk. Timmons shook his head and stalked off to get it.

"Can I go, Chief?" Denise sniffled.

"Yeah." Active put away his notebook. "Do you have someone you can stay with tonight? I don't think you should stay by yourself."

Denise nodded. "I could call my auntie."

"Danny, would you walk Ms. Sheldon to her vehicle? I'm going to take another look at that room."

Paul Noyakuk's temporary hideout looked like any other hotel room. In the bathroom, the towels were neatly folded and untouched. A half-smoked cigarette floated in the toilet, though there was no knowing if it had belonged to Noyakuk or to the housekeeper. A TV remote lay on the floor next to the nightstand. The pillow on that side of the bed was dented, like someone had just started to lean back and get comfortable before being interrupted, maybe by the knock of an irritated guest from next door.

Active lifted the spread and spied an object on the floor between the nightstand and the bed. An empty rifle cartridge box.

His phone warbled with a call from Kavik.

"Chief, Denise's Jeep is gone."

"Was it locked?"

"Yeah. But it wasn't broken into. She locked herself out with her kid in the car about a week ago. So Paul Noyakuk put an extra key on a magnet in the front wheel well for her."

Active poured a cup of coffee from the second pot he had made in the last couple of hours and stretched his arms over his head. He could hear the soft trill of Kavik's snores on the beaten-up leather couch in the reception area outside his office.

They had driven every street in the village, probed with head-lights and flashlights behind every building and dumpster, for three hours of the moonless night, all with no sign of a dark blue Jeep Wrangler. How did somebody hide a Jeep in Chukchi? Finally, with a dense autumn fog starting to roll in on the west wind, Active decided to wait for daylight, still a couple of hours off.

It was 5 A.M. on his desk clock when Kavik shuffled in like a mummy come to life. The smell of the coffee must have roused him.

"I have to take a leak," he said, "then I'll spell you so you can catch a few z's."

Active's eyelids kept falling shut as he waited for Kavik. Then he was behind the wheel of his Tahoe with Grace beside him. Her abdomen was huge. She was crying out in pain every time a contraction hit.

"We've got to get to the hospital for the appointment," he heard himself say.

"Turn left," Grace said. "No, turn right, turn left, turn right." He was speeding through Chukchi, corner after corner, but getting nowhere. Where had the hospital gone?

His chest was pounding. Was this a heart attack? How would he take care of Grace? And the baby? But, no, the appointment—

"Chief, Chief."

Kavik's voice brought him out of it. He lifted his head off his folded arms on the blotter and willed his eyes open. Outside his office window, dawn was lightening the fog in the street. Kavik stood in front of his desk with a young white couple.

"These are the Franklins, Melissa and Joe. They have some information."

Active sat up straight, rubbed his face until he could feel it again, took a gulp of cold, stale coffee, and shook himself to a semblance of alertness.

"Have a seat, please. What's going on?"

"It was about fifteen minutes ago, we were driving out the Loop Road to pick blueberries before work," Joe said, hands and voice shaking. "When we got to the other end of the bridge, there was this vehicle stopped in the middle of the road, facing us, blocking the whole way. I waited a minute or two, honked my horn, but nothing. He didn't move."

"So I told Joe, maybe there's something wrong with the driver," Melissa chimed in. "Like he had a stroke or an engine problem."

Her husband nodded. "So I open my door and I get out and I yell, 'Hey, buddy, you okay?' That's when—"

"I told you not to get out." Melissa put a hand on Joe's thigh. "I told him not to get out, but of course he didn't listen. He never listens."

"So the guy opens his door, points a rifle at us. Blam! Blam! Two shots right over our heads."

"You weren't hit?"

Joe shook his head. "No, but we were scared shitless."

"I screamed out loud," Melissa said. "Right out loud. And I spilled our coffee. The whole thermos."

"I dropped my phone on the road," Joe said. "I didn't even stop to pick it up. I told Melissa to get down. I threw the car in reverse and we got the hell out of there."

Active was on his feet, punching buttons on his phone. "What kind of vehicle?"

"Jeep."

"Dark blue," Melissa added.

"One occupant?"

"Just the driver," Joe said. "Native guy in a camo jacket."

CHAPTER TWENTY-SIX

Active stopped his Tahoe at the east end of the bridge. Kavik pushed a button on the console between the seats and flipped back a locking coil to release an assault rifle from its bracket. He passed it to Active, then gripped his own weapon propped beside him.

They wore stiff black bulletproof vests with CHUKCHI PSD printed on the chests and backs. Alan Long and another officer were parked two car lengths back. Behind them was another blue-and-white with two more officers. Fifty feet beyond that, back where the bridge started, an ambulance stood by on the side of the road, lights flashing.

Active pushed open his door and took cover behind it. Thirty yards ahead, Denise's Jeep sat silent and menacing in the middle of the road. The early morning light was still dim in the fog, but Active could see a man's head moving behind the wheel. The driver's door was open a crack wide enough for a rifle barrel to fit between door and frame, but no weapon was visible.

"Paul Noyakuk!" Active yelled over the Tahoe's PA system. "Get out of the vehicle slowly and put your weapon on the ground! Nobody needs to get hurt here!"

"Fuck you!" Noyakuk shouted back. His head was partially obscured by the outer frame of the windshield and one foot was out the door, moving back and forth on the pavement in a nervous pivot. Now a rifle barrel appeared in the space between the door and the frame, muzzle pointed upward.

"I've got a shot at his foot," Kavik said from behind his door on the passenger side.

"Not yet," Active said. "We do that, he may go down shooting."

Active brought up the two officers at the rear to fire a volley of twelve-gauge bean bags at the Jeep. Two bags thudded into the hood and another took out a headlight. Two others found their mark almost simultaneously at the center of the Jeep's windshield. The glass shattered, drawing a burst of profanity from Noyakuk.

He pulled his leg and rifle inside the rig and shielded his face with his arms in apparent anticipation of more beanbags. The rifle was out of his hands for now, and more of him was visible with the windshield gone. Time for a kill shot?

Active looked at Kavik, who raised his eyebrows in the *naluaqmiut* expression of inquiry. Active shook his head and focused on the Jeep.

"Come on, Paul. We're running out of time here. Get out of the vehicle slowly and put down that weapon."

"Fuck you!" Noyakuk chucked a triangle of glass through the hole where the windshield had been.

Active waited for Noyakuk's next move, but none came. He could hear Kavik breathing on the other side of the Tahoe. His cell warbled from the seat and a Nome number came up. He took the information from the trooper dispatcher there.

"The troopers have a negotiator standing by in Nome if this drags on," he told Kavik. "But this fog's supposed to last a while. He may not be able to get in."

Kavik flexed his shoulders. His eyes remained fixed on the Jeep.

Active connected his cell to the Tahoe's Bluetooth, and punched in Noyakuk's number. Over the SUV's speaker, he heard the other phone click online, then labored breathing.

"Paul, you hear me?"

No answer.

"It's Chief Active. This is a bad deal we got here. How it goes depends on you."

A dry cough answered him.

"I need for you to get out right now, lay your rifle on the ground, then step away from it and show us your hands."

"Yeah, right." Noyakuk's voice was hoarse and monotone, as if from sleep deprivation. "I know I'm dead as soon as I get out. I'm not some dumbass."

"Of course not," Active said. "You're as smart as they come. Who else could bring down an airplane with a couple of balloons?"

Noyakuk was silent for a half minute. Then, "Took me a while to Eskimo that one up, all right."

Active and Kavik exchanged glances. Kavik hooked a quick thumbs-up.

Active cleared his throat and swallowed to relax it. "Listen, how'd you figure that out, anyway? You see the weather lady down at the airport launching her balloons or something?"

"Not at first. Before her, it was them hajis."

"Hajis? What—hajis?"

"In Iraq. Them hajis, they always ride around on their Yamaha motorcycles. One night a couple of 'em that worked on our base put a bunch of inner tubes from them motorcycles in the fuel tanks of one of our Apaches and pumped them up. It run out of gas and hit a cliff and kill fourteen of our people."

"Wow, that must have been tough, but—

"I knew that doctor kill my little girl, he like to fly, but where I'm gonna get that many inner tubes and how I'm gonna have time to pump them up? Then I seen that *taaqsipak* girl with her balloons and it clicked, yeah, that could work on a plane. Way easier than inner tubes, and faster too if I use water instead of air. So I got some balloons online, and waited, thinking about how to do it. Then I see on the Lienhofer schedule he's going to Fairbanks with Cowboy so I get Jesse to let me work for him that night. It was easy."

Active whistled in fake appreciation. "Pretty smart, all right. So, Paul, look. How about you be smart again right now and lay down that gun so we can end this without you or any of my people getting hurt? What do you say? Corey still has his Unca Paw and your mom still has her son, ah? I mean, with that stroke and all, she needs you more—"

"Why should I trust you, *naluaqmiiyaaq*?"

"I'm giving you my word."

"Maybe I trust your Inupiat word, but I don't trust your *naluaqmiiyaaq* word."

"There's good and bad in every color, Paul. I'm sure Dr. Brenner did the best he could with your daughter. He helped a lot of people in Chukchi—*aanas*, little kids, everybody."

"Yeah, but not my kid. He kill her. 'Eye for an eye,' like in the Bible, ah?"

"Where's the eye for an eye for Evie Kavoonah? What did she do to deserve dying like that? She had a family that loved her. And she was carrying a baby."

The Tahoe's speakers went silent for a minute. Then came a gulping sound, like Noyakuk was trying to choke back sobs.

"I didn't know Evie was gonna be in that plane. I wouldn't hurt her. It was supposed to be that Cowboy Decker. That's what the schedule said."

"And you thought it would be okay if he died?"

"Collateral damage, man. Like that school we hit from our drones. I try to tell them *naluaqmiut.*"

"What about Jesse? Was he collateral damage, too?"

"You got no right to talk about him that way!" Noyakuk was crying now. "I loved Jesse. I loved him. That guy was the best friend I ever had."

"Pretty good friend, all right, to put himself at risk to help you do a murder."

"He didn't have nothin' to do with it. All I did was help him get drunk that day, then say I'd work for him so I could be the one fueling up the planes that night. And he sure wasn't gonna tell nobody until you talk to him and he start thinking I never do it right. So he blame himself for not being there to do his job and then it get them people killed, that's what he think. That was his big confession he was gonna make—that he skipped out on work and I gassed up that plane."

"So you killed him."

"No! You killed him! If you never question him, he'll never be dead. It's on you, man! Fuck you, I'm done!"

The phone went silent except for the call's muted static.

"Listen, Paul," Active said. "Let me call the hospital and see if your mom can talk. Okay?"

"Fuck you, *naluaqmiiyaaq*. Don't talk about my mom no more."

Silence. Active waited again. He told Kavik to call the hospital and ask about getting Esther on the phone.

Kavik dialed, spoke, and waited.

The minutes ticked past. Active studied the silent Jeep.

Kavik said "Thanks," and tapped off the hospital call. He looked at Active and shook his head. "The doc says no way, not in her condition."

Active looked at the Jeep again. The longer this went on, the more unraveled Noyakuk would become. He probably hadn't eaten or slept since at least the day before.

And now he was boxed in. A trooper Suburban had come up from the south along the Loop Road and two troopers were now in position fifty yards behind the Jeep. Would Noyakuk give in or try to ram his way out?

"Paul, the doctor says your mom's asking for you," Active lied over the PA. "Let's go see her in the hospital. She needs her—"

"Fuck you, I said don't talk about her."

"Danny," Active called across the seat after several minutes of silence from Noyakuk. "Let's get him out of that Jeep."

Kavik pulled the paintball gun from its storage box in the back of the Tahoe and loaded it with eight red and white pepper balls. He laid the barrel across the door frame and popped off the balls. Four of them sailed into the driver's seat of the Jeep. White fog filled the interior.

Noyakuk leaned out of the Jeep, steadied his rifle on the door hinge and started firing. Bullets pinged off the corner of the Tahoe's windshield frame beside Active's head. Another round slammed into the door he was using for a shield. Something—the armrest, probably—banged into his thigh hard enough that he nearly lost his balance.

He repositioned his AR-15 on the window frame and added his fire to the hail of bullets from Kavik's gun. He sensed another officer moving up on his left and firing a handgun. Bullets pocked the Jeep's hood.

As Active fired off another round, Noyakuk's head bounced up from behind the steering wheel. The driver's door of the Jeep swung wide open.

Active raised his hand and yelled, "Cease fire!"

He waited, crouched behind the Tahoe door, his weapon balanced on the frame of the opened window, his eyes trained on the driver side door of the Jeep, his heart thumping against the bulky vest, the bruised thigh burning.

An arm emerged from behind the Jeep door, holding the rifle and pointing it straight up. Then Noyakuk slowly planted one foot, then the other, outside the Jeep and stepped from behind the door, every law-enforcement gun at the scene following him as he moved. He was completely visible now, arms over his head like he was surrendering, but still with the rifle in one hand, still pointing it at the sky.

Active gathered his breath and shouted. "That's great, Paul. Now just drop your weapon and—"

Noyakuk jerked the rifle into his body and put his mouth over the muzzle. The blast was brief and sharp. A fountain of blood sprayed from the back of his head. He toppled forward and fell face down on the gravel shoulder, arms still cradling the rifle.

Wisps of gun smoke and pepper spray wafted out of the Jeep

and spun away into the fog. Active leveled his weapon at the figure on the gravel and took a step toward the Jeep.

The pain in his thigh blazed up into his abdomen and he had to prop himself against the fender of the Tahoe to keep from going down.

He steadied himself for a few seconds. Sweat poured into his eyes and blurred his vision. He looked down: there at his feet was what looked like his own AR-15. But how could that be?

He looked up and realized people were lined up along the edge of the lagoon, cell phones pointed at him and the scene on the bridge, and he thought how this would be all over Facebook and how he and Nita and Grace would watch the video together and how many views it would get. Then Kavik was beside him. Why was he here?

"Jesus, Chief, you're hit."

Active put his hand on his burning thigh. Something warm pulsed out through his fingers. He looked at it. It was red and it smelled like metal.

Then he was limping toward the ambulance, leaning on Kavik's shoulder as paramedics rushed forward with a stretcher. Kavik sat with him in the back of the ambulance while he was hooked up to an IV.

He came out of it a little, grimaced with the movement of the vehicle and looked up at Kavik. "Nice work out there."

"Easy, Chief," Kavik said. "We'll have you fixed up in no time. I caught Grace at the airport, she's gonna meet us at the hospital."

"She had the poinmen—the appoint—thuh . . ."

CHAPTER TWENTY-SEVEN

Everything above him was gray and flowing, but Active was pretty sure he wasn't underwater. Cold air brushed his face. He heard Grace talking. Her voice was higher than usual—he couldn't make out the words. Then he was being hoisted through a rounded doorway, head first.

"Don't worry, Grace," somebody said in Cowboy's voice. "I've done a hundred medevacs in worse shit than this."

"Medevac?" Active thought the word, but wasn't sure it came out. "Cowboy?"

Whatever he was strapped to jerked and stopped moving. Cowboy's face swam into view above him.

"Hey, buddy, thanks for screwing up my morning," Cowboy said. There's an air ambulance standing by in Nome, but they can't get in with this fog. So, you've got me instead. We'll bust up through this soup and have you in Anchorage before lunch."

"I got shot," Active said, maybe to Cowboy, maybe to himself.

He blinked and forced his eyes into focus. He was inside a plane, that was it, and he was horizontal. Someone hovered over him and fiddled with an IV bag.

Somebody else was picking up his hand. He breathed in lavender and came out of it again, just a little.

"How you doing, baby?" Grace's eyes swam into focus. No quicksilver there now.

"Can't feel much." He tried to smile and squeeze her hand but didn't know if he succeeded.

"Of course not," she said. "You're full of major drugs." She was kneeling beside him, leaning over him, hair brushing his cheeks. "Relax and enjoy, you're gonna be fine."

The door slammed shut and the air inside the plane became still. Cowboy settled into the pilot's seat and barked out words Active couldn't decipher.

The whine of an engine was building up. Another joined in. Two engines, this must be the Nava—Nava—what was it? Navigator? No, Navajo, that was it. He tried to hold his gaze on Grace's eyes, but they wobbled in and out of focus. "I'm sorry, baby," he said. "We need to talk about something, what is it?"

"It's all right," she said. "We can talk later."

Appointment. They needed to talk about an appointment. He tried to say it, but he wasn't sure it came out. His mouth didn't seem to be working now. And his eyelids, how could they be this heavy, like they had weights on them?

"I canceled it," she said.

Apparently he had said it, then, but what appointment?

"I want you to feel something."

He could hear her, but he couldn't see her now.

"The baby moved this morning. Here . . ."

His hand was being lifted again and then held against something soft and warm and curved.

"And then Danny called me, and I realized this is a piece of you. Maybe the only piece I'll—" Her voice caught. "I'm keeping the baby."

The plane was bouncing now. He was light and rising, like a balloon. Her voice faded to a distant and unintelligible buzzing.

He was flying on his back. Swaths of misty clouds buffeted him as he passed through them. Shouldn't he have his arms out? They were pinned to his side—not very aerodynamic. But he was flying.

His eyes drifted up to a window. Still gray out there, but getting lighter now, and now blue, the perfect brilliant blue of endless sky that always waited above the clouds.

His breathing slowed to nothing, too much work now, and the throb of his heart faded away. Was this the big empty? Maybe it wouldn't be that bad. He was dancing through cloud canyons now, like that girl pilot. What was her name?

He shut his eyes. He stopped flying and floated. Five seconds might have passed, or five hours. He felt nothing inside, only a calmness.

She was keeping the baby?

A rapid beeping broke the quiet. Then a stream of tinny, agitated speech that sounded like "Bleeding again . . . nicked the femoral, but . . ." Then, "pressure . . ." The words were lost in the gentle air brushing over his face, and soon he was in the clouds again.

"Oh, Nathan, oh, baby . . ." Her voice was urgent and small and far away.

"Grace," he whispered. He was pretty sure it came out.

He should tell her it wouldn't be so bad, the big empty, then she would stop crying. It was too late now, though. He was floating faster, down through the canyons into that beckoning emptiness.

Then he felt a tiny flutter, an impossibly delicate quiver, against his palm on that soft, warm curve.

There it was again.

And again.

He took a breath and smelled lavender.

His eyes flew open.

"Baby," he said.

And he smiled.

ACKNOWLEDGMENTS

The authors wish to express their heartfelt gratitude to the following people, whose support and assistance made this book possible:

John Creed, Myles Creed, and Susan Andrews, for sharing their expertise about life in the Alaska bush and their knowledge of the Inupiaq language, and for their many other kindnesses in helping bring this story to life.

Mark Borchardt, a bush pilot in the finest sense of the word, for ride alongs over the Alaskan Arctic.

Rick Smart and Keith Jones for their invaluable tutoring on the operation of airplane fuel systems.

Norm Hughes, Eric Swisher, and the other men and women of the Kotzebue Police Department, for much useful information on how policing works in the Alaska bush, and for ride alongs on patrol on spring evenings in the Arctic.

Jim Evak of Kotzebue, for his help with the Inupiaq language and many other particulars of life in the Arctic.

And friends, family members, and fellow writers too numerous to name who reviewed the manuscript along the way and recommended countless improvements.